Unmask

Hooked #6

Charity Parkerson

--Warning: This book is intended for

readers over the age of 18.

Editor: Hercules Editing and Consultants

Photographer: Strangeland Photography

ISBN-10: 1-946099-13-9
ISBN-13: 978-1-946099-13-6

Introduction

Adam wasn't looking for love when it fell in his lap. He doesn't want it.

When Adam landed an internship with *the* makeup artist for the stars, he thought he was on the verge of having all his dreams come true. There was no way he could foresee the nightmare the position would become. By one month in, he wonders if he hasn't made the biggest mistake of his life. That is, until he meets Kano Aramante, the founder of the largest fashion magazine in the world.

Kano doesn't let people in. He learned long ago his position invites users and ladder climbers into his life. Not to mention, *Today's Beauty* is his whole world. He doesn't have time for lovers or friends. Meeting Adam reminds him what it's like to have passion and drive for something just out of reach. He sees so much of himself in Adam, but giving Adam the opportunity of a lifetime turns out to be Kano's biggest mistake.

Adam doesn't mean to fall in love with Kano. The man is too much to resist. His giving nature and powerful presence draw Adam in against his better judgment. They click. But Adam doesn't want to be seen as the man who slept his way to the top. He's worked too hard to have his dreams belittled. It seems no matter how hard they fight to be closer, the gap between Kano and Adam widens. Sometimes, there is no middle ground, and love isn't always enough to conquer all.

Chapter 1

A solid month of interning for *the* world's most famous makeup artist for the stars had taught Adam one thing. This was hell. Hands down. There was no other person on Earth as horrible as Rylan Santos. He'd stripped Adam of every ounce of style, until he was a pasty version of himself— clay for the man's molding. They worked somewhere different almost every day under the most extreme circumstances. Sometimes their small team of five had to get up to fifty models ready to go in under half an hour. They worked runway shows and magazine shoots. Morning shows and award shows. He'd never dreamed he'd meet so many famous people for three minutes at a time and hate so many people in even less. For three weeks now, he'd listened to the importance of today's event. It seemed *Today's Beauty* was a once-a-year and once-in-a-lifetime opportunity for Team Rylan. Its holiday edition shot in October to ensure all photos were ready to go by December first. Every model had to be perfect and several of the magazine's key staff members were involved as well. Since it only came around once a year, and Rylan's interns were on a yearly rotation, this would be Adam's one and only time to shine. Or so he'd been told about a million times.

For Adam, the shoot was like every other one before it. He'd start one model before being pulled to work another. He didn't think he'd completed an entire face in the month he'd been interning for Rylan. The man was brutal. He hated everything Adam did and made sure to tell him. Adam had learned to take it with a grain of salt, since it seemed everyone he worked with hated every little thing about every little thing in the whole world. No need to take it personally. The only difference between this shoot and every other one Adam had worked on in the past was the magazine itself. He'd grown up reading and loving *Today's Beauty*. It was the leading magazine in the world and for good reason—it was the best. They gave the best tips and Adam could credit some of their articles with a few of the tricks he used. He was beyond excited to work with them. Each time the elevator doors opened, bringing with it a new wave of faces, Adam's gaze swung that way, excited to see who he'd spot next.

He'd already seen two pop stars, a super model who looked every bit as good at fifty as she had at twenty, three major actresses, and a guy who'd become famous for being the first out and proud rugby player. Adam had never been more torn between getting to make these people look their best, and getting thrown out on his ass for begging for autographs. The elevator dinged, alerting him of new arrivals and snagging Adam's attention. This time, only two men stepped out. One was large—like basketball player tall and body builder thick. His gaze swept the room as if searching for any threat and ready to kill it. He was intense. Since Adam didn't recognize him, he focused on the second man. Even from feet away, he couldn't miss the man's light-gray eyes— like steel. Adam had never seen the man before, but he screamed power. He was tall too, but not as tall as the first guy. Plus, this man had lean muscle—like a runner. He carried himself like a man who knew his worth and expected everyone else should know it as well. Indeed, people scrambled to clear a spot for him and see to his every need.

The man's gaze flickered Adam's way and lingered. Heat rushed to Adam's cheeks as he realized he'd been caught staring. He tore his gaze away and focused on Chrissy. He was almost finished with her cheekbones, and if he made it that far, she'd be the first model Rylan had let him complete without complaint. It felt a lot like a win to Adam. No matter how hard he tried, Adam kept focusing on the man in the expensive suit. He felt like they'd met somewhere before, even though he knew for a fact they'd never met. The man was familiar in some way Adam couldn't pinpoint. Their gazes met and held once more. This time, Adam didn't blush, but he did look away. There was no time in his life for making eyes across the room, especially with someone out of his league. He needed to get on with things within reach.

*

Kano fucking hated this yearly shoot. He shouldn't. There was nothing on this planet he loved more than his magazine, but he'd never intended to be inside the pages. Unfortunately, ten years ago, some marketing person had suggested doing a holiday edition where people behind the scenes would be featured. He'd seen her logic. Readers loved connecting with the faces behind the products they loved. He'd agreed. It had been a smashing success. Now, he was stuck getting painted up and photographed alongside the models every fucking year. He really fucking hated it. Almost as much as he hated Rylan Santos. The artist for the stars was a necessary evil. He was good at his job and everyone wanted his services. Basically, anyone who was anyone had Rylan work their shoots and shows. Since Kano was somebody, Rylan was his man. That didn't mean Kano needed the man himself doing Kano's makeup. Rylan always made him look like a fucking pasty-arse clown.

11

The instant he'd stepped off the lift, Kano had set his sights on finding a different member of the man's team to do his makeup. A young man around twenty caught his eye. Maybe the man hadn't snagged Kano's attention for the right reasons, but he had it. He was small— skinny and around five-ten. Kano felt certain they'd have to lower his chair so the man could reach him, but for some odd reason, Kano couldn't stop staring at him. There was something about him. Kano didn't understand it. He was drawn to the man. The man's jade eyes kept moving Kano's way. Twice now, he'd held Kano's stare. Kano was intrigued.

Rylan spotted him waiting his turn and rushed to Kano's side. Panic rose in Kano's chest. He put his hand up, stopping the man. "I don't want you touching me. You're fantastic with the models, but you made me look like a trollop last year and had people wondering if I was sick. That chap right there can help me," Kano said, pointing out the young guy working nearby he'd been watching.

Rylan looked scandalized. Not that Kano cared. He paid the man a huge amount to show up when he needed him. That should be all the excuse Kano needed to have his way.

"Adam is just an intern."

Kano held on to his patience by a thread and settled his most scornful stare on Rylan. "Good, then he'll do as he's told."

Although Rylan's eyes flashed with anger, he turned away and called for the artist Kano requested. "Adam, you're ruining Chrissy's face. Come do this chair instead."

Kano's irritation spiked. Rylan's pride was out of control. He checked Adam's reaction. The lad's face remained smooth of all emotion as he switched places with Rylan. "Yes, sir."

For some reason Kano couldn't explain, his hackles rose over Adam's response. It wasn't Adam's voice causing his reaction. The boy had the sweetest southern accent Kano had ever heard. It caressed Kano's ears. Kano didn't like the boy bending to Rylan's will. He didn't know why, but it made his skin feel too tight. Instead of snapping Rylan in two on a day his services were needed, Kano focused on Adam instead.

"I don't like wearing makeup. Don't make me look as if I'm slathered in it."

Adam's mouth lifted in one corner. His jade eyes moved over Kano's features as if staring at a blank canvas and imagining a masterpiece. The rest of the room disappeared. Kano's focus was held captive.

"No one likes makeup. Not really," Adam said, fucking Kano's ears again with his gorgeous voice. "Some people are addicted to how it makes them feel—the way it gives them a mask to hide behind, but deep down, they hate their need for it. But, not everyone has your natural beauty," Adam said. His gaze flickered to Kano's before skirting away again.

Kano knew it wasn't Adam's intention to flirt. The loving note to the man's voice was pride in his work. Kano would know that tone anywhere. He used the same one every time he spoke about *Today's Beauty* at any event. This magazine was his life. His most precious commodity. He'd chosen correctly in Adam. This man wouldn't let Kano go in front of the camera looking anything other than his best. While Adam worked, Kano stared at him. He was young—way too young for Kano's gut to twist with desire the way it was with

Adam touching him. There was a tiny mark on Adam's nose where he'd obviously once had a nose ring. There was one above his eyebrow as well. It looked older, as if he hadn't worn an earring there in years, but the one on his nose... Kano could picture this man with a tiny diamond resting there. Kano also wasn't surprised they were gone. Rylan didn't permit any type of unique expression among his interns. He liked to mold them into faded versions of himself.

"You're going way too light on the eye liner, Adam. Mr. Aramante's eyes are his best feature. Highlight them."

Adam didn't as much as glance Rylan's way. His expression never shifted, keeping his thoughts hidden.

Kano's irritation rose. He'd asked for Adam specifically because he hadn't wanted a heavy hand. "Do it your way," Kano ordered.

Adam's gorgeous gaze met his. A smirk touched his lips. Kano's mouth went dry. "Don't worry, Mr. Aramante. I always do things my way. Also, your eyes aren't your best feature. They're amazing, but not your best."

"Kano."

A line appeared between Adam's eyes. He met Kano's gaze once more. "Excuse me?"

"My name is Kano. You may call me that."

Adam smiled. "Okay." Kano's breath caught at the sight of the man's gorgeous lips curling into a sexy grin. Everything about Adam screamed youth, except his smile. That was sex and heated kisses. "You're finished. Give me your thoughts and don't hold back. I'm thick skinned." He spun Kano's chair, turning him toward the mirror and stealing the sight of Adam's gorgeous face from him.

Kano focused on his reflection instead. "Flawless." The word slipped from Kano without thought, but it was true. There was the barest hint of makeup in just the right places. It was enough the camera wouldn't wash him out, while highlighting his best features. "You're a true artist." Kano's gaze flickered to Adam's in the mirror in time to catch the man's blush. The need to corrupt and control rose inside Kano like an unexpected tsunami. He needed to walk away now before he destroyed this child.

Kano stood. "Thank you, Mr...."

"Adam."

The darkness disappeared. A smile exploded across Kano's face. "Your name is Adam Adam?"

Adam chuckled, tightening Kano's groin. "It's Adam Melkin, but you can call me Adam, Kano."

He recognized Adam had intentionally

used his first name, pointing out the fact Kano had given him permission to do so. Now, if Kano chose not to use Adam's first name, it would be an insult. "Very well, Adam Melkin," Kano said, refusing to be maneuvered. "Thank you for not making the media spend the next year debating if I'm dying of some dreaded disease or just aging badly, as Rylan did last year. Owning a fashion magazine already opens me up to constant judging."

Adam blinked and his expression transformed, closing off and distancing himself from Kano. Realization struck. Adam hadn't known who he was.

*

As far as nights went, Adam hadn't yet decided if this one had been a roaring success or an unmitigated disaster. He'd gone from the quivering fear of retribution when Kano had requested his services over Rylan's, which would no doubt be swift and everlasting, to dancing with joy over the prospect of working on such a beautiful man. Several times, he'd caught himself on the verge of flirting. His cheeks heated at the thought. No doubt Kano thought he was ridiculous. A man like him would never look twice at someone like Adam. That wasn't insecurity talking. Adam knew he had looks on his side. He came from good genes. This was a matter of social standing. Adam was the young intern. Kano was the owner of the world's largest fashion magazine. Now that had come as a huge surprise. He'd known the man had power dripping from his pores, but he'd had no real clue.

If Adam thought Rylan would make his life miserable over a model, that was nothing compared to Kano choosing him. Damn, the man was beautiful. Adam hated to put any makeup on him whatsoever. A growl rose in Adam's head.

This place, he loved it and hated it. He'd always been his own person. Here, he was a station in life. Even if he reached his goals, he'd still be a joke if paired with someone like Kano. They would be the equivalent of an actor dating his kid's nanny. Normally, something like this would roll off his skin. He wasn't in New York to find a man. Adam was here to chase a dream—to succeed. Men came and went, taking what they wanted. He'd seen it time and time again with his uncle, Jace. He'd promised himself he'd learn from that and stay true to himself. At the end of the day, all Adam had was himself. He was the only person who would never leave him. His dreams mattered more than a love affair that would end as quickly as it began. Adam had bigger expectations from life. Still, those steel-gray eyes had been amazing, especially when they focused on Adam. Jesus. He was an idiot.

Adam went back to cleaning up his work station. They needed to be ready to go for a shoot tomorrow morning, and nothing was more irritating than not being able to find what he needed because they'd left everything unorganized the day before. Plus, concentrating on the mundane calmed him. It was Adam's equivalent of meditation. Everything had its place. Brushes in one spot. Eyeshadow in another. Toners stick together.

"It's incredibly tacky to flirt with the boss."

Adam's shoulders fell at the sound of Rylan's nasally voice. "I never flirt," Adam said, keeping his gaze locked on his task. It was true. Even when Adam liked someone, he refused to give them that sort of power.

Rylan scoffed. "Bullshit. We all do. It's how we survive. We use our beauty to get our way and stay on top. If you don't believe that, you're in the wrong business."

"If you say so," Adam said, keeping his tone bland. Rylan loved drama. No good could come of engaging.

"You shouldn't bother coming in tomorrow."

Adam straightened away from his task. He kept his features carefully blank as he turned. "Excuse me?"

Rylan's evil smile let him know he hadn't heard wrong. "It's not your fault. When I first saw you, I thought you had amazing talent. Now I realize my mistake. You don't have what it takes to do this on a permanent basis. That's on me. I shouldn't have chosen you for this. Tomorrow, you needn't bother showing up. This was your last shot. You don't belong here."

Adam couldn't breathe. He'd done his best to keep his head down and stay off

Rylan's radar, but it hadn't been enough. His dream was dead less than five weeks after it began. He'd have to call Jace, and tell the man who'd given him every opportunity in the world that he'd failed.

"He's right," Kano said, appearing out of nowhere. "You don't belong here. Your place is on the twenty-sixth floor, which is where you'll meet me at eight a.m. sharp." He buttoned his jacket without meeting anyone's stare. Adam wanted to beg the man to look at him. Kano headed for the elevator, still barking orders. "I realize that's much earlier than you're accustomed to, working in this department, but I keep to a different schedule. Give your address to my driver. He'll pick you up and save you from the early morning rush."

Adam scrambled after him—Rylan all but forgotten in the wake of Kano's announcement. "I'm sorry. Did I miss something? What's on the twenty-sixth floor? Who is your driver? I have no idea what's happening."

Kano waved him onto the elevator. "This lift won't wait all night, Adam."

Adam jumped inside before he got left behind.

Kano motioned toward the bull-sized man who'd stepped off the elevator with Kano earlier. "This is my driver, Tim. Give him your address."

Adam dutifully rattled off directions to his apartment as his mind raced. He'd gone from fired to the unknown in a matter of seconds, and now he was off balance. "What's on the twenty-sixth floor?"

Kano smirked. "My office. I hope you have a passport."

Adam shook his head.

An exasperated-sounding sigh escaped Kano. "We'll work on that tomorrow. Thankfully, we have a little time left before I'm scheduled to be in London."

"I'm confused," Adam admitted. He still had no clue what was happening.

"I've given you a job, Mr. Melkin. A real, paying means of employment. I do interviews all over the world. You're the first makeup artist who did as I asked. That means you now do it on a full-time basis. Where I go, you go."

"Am I Mr. Melkin now?" Adam wanted to bite his tongue. He wasn't trying to be a smart ass. Adam genuinely needed to know where he stood.

Kano ignored him. "I have a TV interview in Los Angeles tomorrow. Be ready to leave when Tim picks you up. We'll be gone three days. Pack accordingly and clear your schedule."

"I'm working at a department store the day after tomorrow. It's how I pay my bills."

Kano's gaze locked on Adam, making him want to squirm. "Is seventy-five thousand a year enough to cover your rent?"

"That's... Yes."

"It's settled then. I'll see you tomorrow, Adam. Don't be late," Kano said, stepping from the elevator and leaving Adam standing there, no longer certain of anything.

*

Kano fumed all the way to the car. He always tried letting Rylan run his team with little to no interference, but the man had gone too far today. The idea Rylan would fire Adam simply because Kano had chosen the boy over him was ludicrous. Adam had looked devastated. Rylan— proud of wrecking someone's dreams. If Kano hadn't appeared when he had, it would've happened. How many others had suffered the same fate? Rylan worked hard for Kano when he hired him for shoots. He wasn't sure what to do about the man long term, but he knew without a doubt he wouldn't allow Rylan to damage someone with as much talent as Adam. His decision had been an impulsive one. Kano didn't regret it.

Tim opened the back door of the black Mercedes-AM G65, waiting for Kano to climb inside. Kano hesitated and met the man's dark gaze. He'd been with Kano for ten years. Kano trusted him with his life—literally, since Tim was actually Kano's bodyguard. Driving was only one of Tim's many hats.

"What would you have done?"

Tim didn't hesitate. "You did the right thing."

With a nod, Kano climbed inside. "I

hope so," he said more for himself. In truth, he wouldn't question his decision if not for the way he'd reacted to Adam touching him. Of course, Tim didn't know that part. Kano wondered if his answer would've been different had Tim known. After all, if anyone would know how Kano hadn't been attracted to anyone in years, it would be Tim. The man was with him almost twenty-four hours a day.

Kano waited until Tim slid behind the wheel before seeking more advice. "What should I do about Rylan? I don't wish to alienate him but neither will I tolerate this cattiness."

"Let me talk to him."

A burst of unexpected laughter hit Kano. "I don't need you to kick his arse."

Tim's voice sounded heavy with laughter when he responded. "No ass kicking. Just talking. I'll take care of things."

"If you so choose," Kano said, happy to pass the job to someone else. He hated confrontation.

"Do you really intend to pay the boy seventy-five thousand a year just to do your makeup before interviews?"

Kano focused on the passing scenery. He'd pulled the figure out of his arse at the spur of the moment. He had no idea what people needed to live in New York these days. Kano had been in white-knight mode and said the first thing that came to mind. "I'll get my money's worth out of him. There's always more for me to do than I have hours in the day."

"That's true."

"Who knows," Kano said, the idea growing on him. "Maybe you can actually have a few days off now and again."

"I wouldn't know what to do with myself." The honesty in Tim's voice gave Kano pause. Sometimes, he didn't think much about his staff's personal lives. He worked. They worked. No one complained, but he was certain Tim might like to have something to do other than being with him all the time. Plus, he liked the idea of being alone with Adam. A little too much.

Chapter 2

Adam waited until he had noodles boiling before calling Jace. He was excited to share his news, but also a little nervous. Jace had helped him move to New York for an internship. A real, paying job felt permanent—like he'd never call Tennessee home again. After setting the phone on the counter, Adam called Jace, and left it on speaker.

Jace answered on the third ring, sounding breathless. "Hello?"

"Hey. Did I catch you at a bad time?"

Jace gasped again. "No."

Adam shook his head. "Okay," he said, drawing out the word. "I have some big news."

"Me too," Jace said, sounding excited and piquing Adam's curiosity.

"You go first," Adam begged, stalling. He still wasn't sure if he was ready to tell

Jace anything.

"Are you sure?"

Adam rolled his eyes, thankful Jace couldn't see him. "Yes. Tell me."

Jace let out a nervous-sounding chuckle, causing Adam to move closer to the phone. Suddenly, he had to know. "Tyler and I got married today," Jace said fast like ripping off a bandage.

"What?" Adam didn't mean for the question to come out sounding accusing. He'd been caught off guard. He scrambled to fix it. "I mean, that's awesome. Tyler seems like a really great guy. Is he around? Put me on speaker so I can congratulate you both."

Jace laughed. He sounded happy in a way Adam hadn't heard him in a long time. A hint of jealousy wormed its way into Adam's heart. He hadn't been happy in a long time either. For a moment, Adam wished there was someone out there for him. He pushed the feeling aside. Jace deserved this. He'd earned a good man by putting up with so many horrible ones. Tyler better stay good or Adam would unman him.

"Hey, Adam. How's big city life treating you?" Tyler asked, his booming voice coming though the line.

Adam smiled at the sound. Tyler was a good man. "It's going great. So, I hear I have a new uncle."

"Yeah," Tyler said, sounding every bit as happy as Jace. "You okay with that?"

Adam didn't hesitate. "Are you kidding me? I'm thrilled. What took you so long?" The sound of Jace and Tyler's laughter over his joke warmed Adam's heart. The pair marrying after only a few weeks of dating might've come as a huge surprise, but life was short. "Does this mean I get to call you Uncle Tyler?"

"Whatever you want."

"Uncle Tyler it is," Adam said, warming up to the idea. "So, did I catch you honeymooning?"

"Yeah, but we're never too busy for you."

Jace cut in. "Speaking of which, what was your news?"

"It can wait," Adam said, chickening out. "It was nothing compared to yours and I want y'all to get back to being alone. You both deserve every happiness in the world." They did, but Adam felt alone all the sudden—like his last connection to another person was slipping away. He didn't have anyone to share his moment with.

"Now you have our curiosity up. You have to tell us." A knock landed on the front door. Adam stared at it in confusion.

"I'll call you when you're back home. Someone's at the door."

"Okay," Jace said, sounding

disappointed.

"Take your Taser with you when you answer," Tyler said over the top of him.

"Okay, guys. Love you," he said as he disconnected the call and moved to check the peephole. Kano stood on the other side. Adam stepped back, gathered his thoughts, and checked again. Yep, it was Kano.

After shoving his phone in his back pocket, Adam pulled the door open. "Kano." Even to his own ears, Adam sounded breathless. "What brings you by?"

"I forgot to get your number, so I didn't have a way to tell you, Rylan usually packs his own supplies. With you being a part of his team, I wasn't sure if you'd have something of that nature."

Adam ran through a list in his head of what he had on hand. "I have a few things."

36

"Come on then, I'll take you to get what you need. Since it's business related, I should be the one paying for it anyhow."

Adam shook his head. "I'm in the middle of making dinner."

"Oh." With one word, Kano transformed into a level of discomfort Adam had never witnessed. It was as if the man was in new waters—like no one had ever disobeyed him.

Adam wasn't now. He just couldn't leave right that second. While chewing his bottom lip, Adam weighed his options. The worst that could happen would be Kano saying no. He stepped back. "Would you like to join me? It's only spaghetti and garlic bread, but it's food. And it's free," Adam tacked on. He blushed as he remembered who he was speaking to. Kano most likely hadn't considered the price of anything in his life.

To his surprise, Kano smiled. Adam's

gaze locked on the gorgeous way the man's lips curled and didn't budge. "I admit, I am famished."

That accent. Adam had to know. "Where are you from?"

Kano unbuttoned his jacket and looked around for a place to put it. Adam relieved him of it. "I'm from Weybridge. It's close to London. What about you?"

"Murfreesboro," Adam said as he moved to hang the coat on a rack behind the door. The material still held the warmth of Kano's body and smelled amazing. He'd never held such an expensive piece of material. It took every ounce of Adam's willpower not to bring the jacket to his nose and inhale Kano's scent. Instead, he focused on their conversation. "It's just south of Nashville, Tennessee."

Kano's smile reappeared. "How many country music artists have you met?"

Adam waved Kano toward the kitchen

as he answered. "None, but that's always the first question people ask when they find out where I'm from. I imagine you've met countless famous people," Adam said as he moved to the kitchen.

Kano followed on his heels. "Yes. Most of them are like everyone else, and still refuse to admit they're famous. Others think everyone should cater to their every whim. I suppose you'll see for yourself soon."

Against his will, Adam's hand shot to his stomach. Nerves set in whenever he thought of this new position. He wasn't sure he was qualified for whatever Kano planned for him. "You haven't said what I'll be doing," Adam said as he stirred the sauce for their spaghetti.

"Mostly you'll be stuck with me. I travel a lot for interviews, and as much as I hate being primped for each one, it's a necessary evil. You'll travel with me. I also have more work to do than any one man should. I'll shift responsibilities to you as they arise."

"So, I'm sort of like a personal assistant with primping skills?" Adam asked, incapable of keeping the laughter from his voice.

"Pretty much," Kano said as he leaned over the counter and eyed the pot Adam stirred. "That smells delicious. Is cooking another of your talents?"

Adam blushed. "Not really. This is one of the few things I can make. Basically, I can cook about four things. Just enough to keep me alive."

Kano's chuckle made the confession worthwhile.

"What about you?" Adam asked. "Do you have any hidden talents, besides having created my all-time favorite magazine?"

"Truly?" Kano's expression said Adam's answer mattered. "Is *Today's Beauty* your favorite or are you saying that because you're talking to me?"

Adam set his spoon aside and gave Kano his full attention. "No. I mean it. I love your magazine. It's been my favorite for as long as I can remember. I even use a few of your beauty tips. You're always on top of every year's fashion. Love it."

Kano's eyes flashed with pride. His smile made Adam's skin feel too tight. "That makes my night."

Adam shook his head. "I should think people tell you all the time how awesome your creation is."

"Only while kissing my arse," Kano said without an ounce of conceit in his tone. "Rarely does anyone say it because they mean it. You did."

"I could've been kissing butt too," Adam said, pointing out the obvious.

"Nah," Kano said, sounding certain. "I get the impression you'd never kiss anyone's arse."

"Given the right circumstances, I might," Adam said under his breath as he pulled the bread from the oven. Kano's roar of laughter let Adam know he hadn't missed Adam's words. Adam blushed again. He wasn't sure what it was about this man that kept him on the edge of embarrassment.

"Can I help in some way?"

At the question, Adam eyed Kano's expensive clothing. "No, thank you. I think I have things under control."

"I'm not afraid of getting dirty," Kano said, as if he read Adam's thoughts, but there was something more in Kano's statement—like it had a double meaning.

Since he genuinely seemed to want to help, Adam nodded toward a cabinet to his left as he carried the boiling pot of noodles to the sink to drain them. "If you'd like, you can grab us a couple of plates."

No sooner than the words left his mouth, Adam felt Kano at his back. His chest brushed Adam's back as he reached past Adam and pulled a couple of plates from the cabinet Adam indicated. In his surprise, Adam dumped the noodles too fast into the colander, causing boiling-hot water to splash onto his wrist.

"Dang," Adam muttered, wincing against the pain.

Kano quickly set the plates aside

before readjusting the faucet to the empty side of the sink and turning the water on cold. He shoved Adam's wrist under the cold water, taking away the sting. Adam kept his gaze locked on his arm. He didn't as much as blink while Kano's gorgeous fingers massaged the reddened spot on his arm.

"Are you okay?" The softly spoken words caressed the shell of Adam's ear.

"Yes," Adam lied. With Kano standing so close—his breath and body touching him, Adam wasn't sure if he'd ever be okay again. Over the years, he'd listened as friends had exclaimed over butterflies and crushes. Adam had only ever been slightly moved by anyone. This man, he set Adam's skin on fire. His boss. A man fifty million light years out of his league. All Kano did was caress Adam's wrist, and Adam's mind already had Kano naked.

This couldn't happen. He couldn't let this happen.

Adam shut the water off and stepped out of Kano's hold. "It's okay now. Thank you." Even to Adam, his smile felt fake.

With a nod, Kano let Adam keep his distance. "Why don't you sit down and take it easy for a minute. Let me finish making our plates."

The pressure in Adam's chest increased at Kano's offer. Why was this man so nice? "You don't know where anything is. I'll do it."

Kano steered Adam toward a barstool at the bar, separating the kitchen from the living room. "Sit," he ordered. "It's not as if your kitchen is so huge I'll never find what I need. I'm used to being in charge. Just sit."

Adam reluctantly did as told. As he

45

watched Kano moving around his kitchen, Adam wondered if he'd fallen down a rabbit hole when he hadn't been looking. This morning, he'd been an invisible intern. Tonight, one of New York's most famous billionaires was making spaghetti in Adam's tiny kitchen. What were the odds?

*

If anyone had ever offered to share their meal with Kano, he couldn't remember it happening. He couldn't get enough of Adam's company. It was almost as if Kano was someone else. Everything he did was out of character. First, he'd offered a job that didn't exist to someone who—most likely—didn't have the resume to match. Now, he was cooking dinner. What the fuck? The man hadn't even cursed when he'd burned himself. Kano barely stopped himself from shaking his head. He had no business alone with someone this innocent and untainted by life. He couldn't stop. Kano hadn't felt so... normal in years.

He glanced Adam's way. There was an ugly red mark forming on the man's wrist. Adam was watching him. Not an ounce of pain etched the man's features, but that detail didn't stop Kano's concern from growing. "Do you have a first aid kit around here?"

Adam shook his head. "I'm fine."

Kano couldn't tear his gaze away from the burn. It looked to him as if it was beginning to swell. "Apologies. I can't take it." Without warning, he urged Adam from his seat and dragged him back to the sink. Kano shoved Adam's arm under the cold water once more. He glanced over. Adam's face was less than two inches from his. Up close, Adam's eyes were even more

47

gorgeous than he'd first thought. At some point, he'd added a layer of eyeliner, making the green pop. Streaks of blue and gold throughout the jade coloration made Adam's eyes the most beautiful and unique Kano had ever seen.

"I may've been wrong earlier," Adam said, sounding as if the admission was more for himself than Kano. "Your eyes might be your best physical feature."

Kano's mind went blank as he realized they'd been thinking about the same thing. "You said earlier they weren't. Now I'm filled with anticipation at hearing what you originally thought was my best feature."

Adam blushed.

Kano forgot why they were standing so close. He tore his gaze away before he made a fool of himself with a much younger man. After lifting Adam's wrist from the water, he inspected the burn closer. He didn't see any blisters forming and no skin appeared to be broken. Still, the wound was near a joint and he was certain he'd heard somewhere that was a bad thing. He pushed Adam's arm back beneath the cool water and pulled out his phone. Kano didn't bother asking for Adam's permission. He was always the one in charge. This situation was no different.

Tim answered on the first ring, just as he was paid to do. "What's up?"

"Adam's burned himself. Send Dr. Jameson."

"Wait. What?" Adam said, looking on the verge of outrage.

"On it," Tim said, disconnecting the call. The man knew Kano well enough not to bother with pleasantries.

"Seriously, Kano, I'm fine," Adam argued the second Kano put away his phone. "This is nothing compared to some of the burns I've suffered from flat irons."

Kano's spine stiffened. No one ever argued with him. "As long as you're working for me, you'll be working by my rules. If I say you need medical treatment, you'll get medical treatment."

"I'm not working for you at the moment. This is my place and I was cooking you dinner, because I'm a nice person and you seem like a nice person. Don't push me into making you leave. If I say I don't need medical treatment, then I don't need it."

They stared each other down. A flush rode high on Adam's cheeks, proving he was on the edge of losing his temper. Kano kind of wanted to see it happen. Adam was a passionate person. Maybe he hadn't used impolite words when he'd burned himself, but he was no pushover either. Kano hadn't felt so alive in years.

"Do you still wish to be my assistant?"

Since Kano had intentionally kept his tone light, as if he could be dissuaded from his decision, Adam looked understandably confused by the question. "I do."

Kano gestured carelessly. "Then you are always on the clock. Since I don't wish to be sued for workman's comp, then you will see my doctor. At my expense, of course," Kano added, in case this was a monetary issue.

"I quit fifteen minutes ago."

A smile tugged at the corners of Kano's mouth. He tried fighting it and lost. "No. You didn't."

Dimples appeared at the corners of

Adam's mouth. Kano's gaze dropped to the man's lips. They were full and sexy, but that smile. Damn. Kano couldn't look away. "Fine. You fired me fifteen minutes ago."

The desire to kiss Adam and taste the man's defiance was a real thing. Kano took a step back, fighting his growing interest.

"I just rehired you." A knock landed on the door, making Kano smirk. "And look, the company doctor is in. Lucky thing I quickly hired you back."

Adam huffed but didn't argue as Kano headed for the door. His hand touched the knob. As if Adam couldn't take not having the final word, he called at Kano's back. "For the record, you didn't win. I'm letting you have your way."

Kano had never been more glad to have his back to anyone. The smile stretching his lips made his face hurt. Maybe Adam didn't think Kano had won, but Kano damn sure felt like a winner, and it had nothing to do with their disagreement.

* * *

Adam had never been on a private plane. Part of him wanted to hate the experience. After this, flying commercial would be miserable. By the third time of him extending his legs all the way because he could, Kano obviously lost patience with his newbie behavior.

Kano sighed and set his phone aside. "Have you ever won a hand of poker?"

Adam shrugged. "I've never played."

Steel eyes watched him with open humor. "That doesn't surprise me. Second question. Why are you no longer wearing your nose ring?"

Adam's face screwed up in confusion.

He couldn't stop it. "How did you know that?"

"I notice everything, Adam, including the minute scar beside your nose. Do you intend to answer me?"

Adam waved away the question. "Rylan said I had to be a blank canvas if I wanted to stay in his program."

"Did you not find it odd for a stylist to expect you to not have style?"

"I don't find anything Rylan does odd, because everything he does is strange," Adam answered, being honest. Rylan was eccentric to say the least. Adam had come to accept the man might do, say, or demand anything.

A smile exploded across Kano's face. Adam's mind went blank. The man's smile was the most amazing thing Adam had ever seen. His breath quickened. Even after being exposed to it for hours the night before, Adam couldn't adjust to the impact of Kano's happiness. "Your logic is sound," Kano said as he picked up his phone and went back to toying with the device, stealing his beautiful gaze from Adam. "Tomorrow, I expect you to go back to being yourself," Kano said without looking at him. "I don't need nor do I want clay to mold."

"Yes, sir."

Kano let out another irritated-sounding sigh but didn't expound. "How's the arm today, by the way?"

Adam glanced down at the white gauze covering his burn. "It's okay. I keep forgetting about it and hitting it on everything."

While staring at his phone, Kano nodded. "Make sure you keep it covered and slather that cream on it every two hours, like the doctor said."

"Yes, sir."

"For fuck's sake," Kano muttered

under his breath, sounding irritated.

Adam looked at Tim for any help figuring out what he'd done wrong.

Tim looked thoughtful as he switched his gaze between them, as if clicking together puzzle pieces in his mind. With a mental shrug, Adam extended his legs again and marveled over how they touched nothing but empty air. A low rumble of laugher caressed Adam's ears, making him smile. He didn't care if Kano found him novice and ridiculous. Adam loved making the prickly man smile. For sanity's sake, he chose not to look at the reason too closely. He didn't have anything to back up his gut feeling, but Adam didn't think Kano smiled often and meant it. Adam would have to do his best to fix that.

By the time they reached the TV station in Los Angeles, the place was buzzing with activity. The moment they arrived on set, they were hustled along.

56

Four people tried talking to Kano at once while the man seemed to somehow understand them all. Adam scurried along behind him with Tim keeping him sandwiched between them, ensuring he didn't get left behind. It seemed quite a few stars brought their personal stylist with them. No one made any noise about being inconvenienced by Adam's presence. They pointed him to an empty station stocked with product.

While Kano handled the circus like a pro, Adam did his best to stay out of the way. He hated feeling useless, but he didn't know what he should be doing. The women working nearby were overwhelmed. Even though Adam was certain they were accustomed to working at a fast pace and under pressure, he wished he could help. He glanced Kano's way. Kano was still busy.

Adam moved closer the red-haired

lady, Hannah, who Kano had introduced as being in charge. "If it's okay with my boss, I could pitch in if you're interested."

Relief filled her bright green eyes. "That would be awesome. We have two extra sets going live this morning for holiday tapings."

Before Adam could respond, Kano turned his way. "Do as you please, Adam. Just don't let it interfere when it's my turn."

Adam blinked at Kano's back. The man had somehow been aware of Adam's every word and move even as he dealt with the set's craziness.

Hannah touched his arm, bringing his attention her way. "You can get started with Tamara over there, if you'd like," she said, pointing toward a platinum blonde. With a nod, Adam jumped into the fray with both feet. It felt good to complete a project with no interference, only exclamations of joy. He made more connections in one day than he'd made in a month of interning for Rylan. Three different people had given him their number for future business. One model had asked him to handle her bridal party for her wedding day. Adam was blown away. If Kano was the least bit annoyed, he never showed it. In fact, he winked the one time he overheard someone offering Adam side work. With that one gesture, Adam had been set at ease. Perhaps this hadn't been the job he'd moved to New York for, but it was amazing nonetheless.

Chapter 3

Two months passed in a blink of an eye. Every day was something different and Adam got to do what he loved. He'd never dreamed his life could be this extraordinary. Before Kano, Adam had been three places: Tennessee, Florida, and New York. Since he'd gone to work for Kano, Adam had visited almost every state and three countries. Kano promised they wouldn't always be traveling this much. It was the holiday season and looming New Year that had them on the go. Everyone wanted to interview Kano about holiday fashion and trends for the upcoming year. The man swore once they made it past the first of January, things would slow and Adam would be bored to tears. Adam had a hard time imagining ever being anything but enthralled in Kano's company. The man was a genius. Adam learned something new every day, making Adam want to hang on the man's every word. He almost hated going home at night. Soon he would head back to Tennessee for Christmas. Although Adam couldn't wait to see Jace, he already missed Kano and they were still together.

"Let's go."

Adam looked up from the makeup kit he was organizing and focused on Kano. "Oh, okay." Adam stood and glanced longingly at his chore. He'd really hoped he could finish tonight. When he got back from his short trip to Tennessee, they'd be off to London again. If it didn't get done tonight. It wouldn't get done. "Where are we headed?" Adam asked as he scrambled after Kano's long stride.

Kano slowed his pace, allowing Adam to catch up before responding. "I like to dive into the craziness of holiday shopping at the mall. I can people watch and check

61

out what everyone's snatching up this year. Plus, I still have to buy gifts."

Adam somehow managed to hold his curiosity at bay until they were walking side by side and dodging the crowd at Brookfield Place. "I've never heard you talk about your family."

"That's because we aren't close," Kano admitted, as if it was a dirty secret. "But they're still my family. That means a short lunch, two days after Christmas, and a perfunctory exchanging of gifts."

"Sounds cold," Adam said without thought.

Kano glanced over with a smile. "Says the chap who intends to only go home for less than a day."

Adam shook his head. "It hasn't been that long since I've seen my family. They came to visit less than a month ago."

A line appeared between Kano's eyes. "I didn't know that. You should've said something. I would've ensured they had the best trip money can buy."

Which was one of the many reasons Adam hadn't said anything. Not only would Kano have taken over Jace's visit, the way he controlled everything, Adam didn't know how to introduce Kano. Calling the man his boss didn't seem sufficient. "It was a quiet visit, on my days off. Now, what do you intend to buy for your family?" Adam asked, changing the subject. This was the closest they'd ever come to discussing Jace and Tyler. Adam intentionally kept his family private. He couldn't explain why. It was as if the more Kano knew, the more pieces of Adam he owned. Adam already had a hard time falling asleep at night. When he closed his eyes, the phantom scent of Kano's cologne surrounded him. The memory of each time Kano had unwittingly touched him that day would run through Adam's mind. He'd question every brush of skin on skin, wondering if it had been intentional. If so, was it Kano or he who'd initiated it?

"My sister, Nina, is an easy one. She likes to travel. I always get her a trip to somewhere new. My parents, they have everything and hate all of it, so—in a way—they're simple as well. I'll never please them, so I can get them whatever. It won't matter."

"How could anyone be disappointed in you? You're the most amazing person I know," Adam said without thought. He didn't take it back. Outrage over anyone thinking less of Kano than he deserved choked Adam. "If I had a son who accomplished a thimbleful of what you've done, I'd be ecstatic."

"If you had a son, you'd be thrilled by everything he did, because you're a good person," Kano said. His eyes danced with laughter. "My parents aren't like you."

Kano's gaze moved to a spot over Adam's shoulder. He grabbed Adam's hand and pulled him to a stop. "Look at that watch." Adam dutifully turned to stare at the blue-faced silver watch in the window of a store he'd never heard of before. "That's a beautiful piece."

"It is," Adam agreed, but his mind was fixed on the way Kano's palm pressed against his, and his thumb lightly stroked the side of Adam's hand. He didn't think Kano was aware of what he was doing. Adam couldn't concentrate on anything else.

"I need to make note of the brand. Watches are coming back. They'd gone out for a while, with everyone using their phones to keep track of the time, but the new fitness-watch trend has brought back the old-feel sensation of checking your wrist instead." Kano released Adam's hand and typed on his phone for a moment as he spoke. After shoving the phone back inside his jacket, Kano reclaimed Adam's hand and resumed walking. "Anyhow, people are paying more for watches these days than ever before."

Adam tried pulling him to a stop. "You should buy it if you like it. I don't mind waiting."

Kano shook his head, but his eyes shone bright. "I'm still one of those who checks the time on my phone."

Adam tore his gaze away from Kano's perfect features and glanced back at the watch. "But that would look amazing on you. Between it matching the color of your eyes and the nice suits you wear, you need that watch."

The grip on Adam's hand tightened. "I'm not sure anyone needs a seven-thousand-dollar watch."

His head jerked around at Kano's words. "Seven thousand dollars? Are you freaking kidding me? No wonder I've never heard of the brand. I've never even owned a car worth seven thousand dollars. Wow. I'd be scared to leave my apartment, thinking I'd get mugged if I wore that watch."

Kano's sexy rumble of laughter made Adam's confessions worthwhile. "What do you want for Christmas?"

You. The admission rang so loudly through Adam's mind, he feared for a moment he'd said the word aloud. Heat filled his cheeks. He glanced away, hoping Kano wouldn't catch his blush. "I don't need anything."

Kano squeezed his hand again, reminding Adam they still held on to each other. "That's not what I asked. Gifts have nothing to do with need. What do you want?"

Adam shrugged. Discomfort set in. He knew if he answered, Kano would ensure

Adam got exactly that, even if he said he wanted a Lamborghini. Adam couldn't decide which would be worse, saying nothing or answering with something small. Either way, he had a bad feeling Kano would buy him something. He deflected instead. "What do you want? What does one buy the man who has everything?"

"I don't have everything."

The seriousness in Kano's voice and stare made Adam realize they'd stopped walking. They stood in the middle of the mall with people pushing past them, staring at each other. He wondered which of them would break first. Adam feared it would be him.

"What's missing from your life?" He shouldn't have asked. Adam needed to know. Someone had to be the first. They were more than they admitted. Here they were, holding hands while Christmas shopping. A boss and his employee didn't do that.

"You are."

There it was. The smile tugging at Adam's lips matched the one in his heart. "No, I'm not. I'm right here."

"Then it's settled," Kano said, walking away and pulling Adam along with him. "My life is complete. I'm officially the man who has everything and is therefore impossible to buy for."

Adam blinked several times, wondering what happened. He very much feared he'd just been maneuvered. Kano knew Adam couldn't afford to buy him a seven-thousand dollar watch, so he'd found a way around answering Adam's question. Dang. Well, at least Adam hadn't had to answer either. Of course, none of that explained why he felt so disappointed.

* * *

Meeting Kano's family was a learning experience. He'd known the man planned to meet them for lunch two days after Christmas. Adam had also known he'd be in London with Kano at the time. What he hadn't known was Kano would expect his presence at lunch. Adam's parents had been the most loving people in the world. When they'd passed, Adam had gone on to be with the greatest uncle ever created. This blessing had never been clearer than now, sitting with the worst people Adam had ever met. The odd thing about it was, they were nice to him—nicer than they were to their son, which wasn't saying much.

"Your cousin Ana says she saw you a few weeks ago on the *Bailey and Basil* show, telling people what to wear to this year's holiday party if they want to catch that co-worker they've had their eye on."

Kano froze with his fork halfway to his

mouth at his mother's words. By his expression, Adam knew Kano expected something awful was headed his way. "Yes."

Judith's eyes flashed—like a woman who smelled blood. Adam couldn't look away. "I told her that was rich, considering you'd never been able to catch a woman. So much so you've turned to men." Everyone laughed, except Kano and Adam. Kano looked resigned.

A lead weight landed on Adam's chest and refused to budge. He'd always been accepted by his family. Maybe not so much by his peers, but his flesh and blood had been there—like nature intended. These people; they were awful. He couldn't take it.

"Actually, there's a receptionist at work who would likely cut off her right arm if Kano ever noticed her advances." All eyes moved his way. The laughter died away. Adam intentionally didn't meet Kano's stare. There was a real chance Adam might not have a job after today, but he couldn't sit quietly through Kano's public humiliation.

"There you go, son," Charles said. "No need to keep embarrassing us with your nancy ways."

Adam's muscles tensed. Never in his life had he wanted to physically fight someone the way he did then. Under the table, Kano squeezed his thigh, as if silently asking him to settle down.

"What Adam meant is," Kano said, capturing everyone's focus. "she doesn't have a chance in hell, because he is the only person holding my interest." As if it had been rehearsed, every head turned his way. Adam couldn't catch his breath. He couldn't decide if it was due to the combined hatred staring his way, or Kano's words.

"Aren't you—"

Adam had no clue what Judith had been about to ask, because Kano cut her off.

"He's here as my guest. Please don't make him feel unwelcome. After all," Kano said, pasting on a bright smile. "He picked out your gifts this year."

"You did?" Nina asked, speaking up for the first time since they'd been seated inside the overpriced posh restaurant. "Brilliant. What did I get?"

Her blue eyes flashed with happiness. They were a few shades darker than Kano's beautiful eyes, but they were shaped the same. Adam thawed a hair. She didn't give him the same spiteful vibe as her parents.

Adam tried for a genuine smile. "Kano told me you love to travel, so I tried thinking of places I've never been but have always dreamed of, and came up with a

73

list. Don't let Kano fool you; he narrowed the list down. I can't believe how many places you've visited. I'm jealous." He knew he was rambling, but even the air was choking Adam. He needed some common ground before he broke under the pressure.

Nina waved away his words. "It's all Kano's doing. I could never afford to travel without his help." Her face hardened as she spent equal time eyeing each parent. "In fact, everyone at this table couldn't afford half what they enjoy without Kano, but you'd think they'd forgotten." Her features softened once more as she focused on Adam. "But I'd love to hear your list. I'm becoming quite the expert on going on holiday." She laughed, as if the thought of being an expert on travel was a joke.

Her statement gave Adam an idea. He turned Kano's way. "You should have a segment in *Today's Beauty* on travel. Something like where the most gorgeous people go, or what to pack on a budget. Something of that nature. Nina could help, and maybe even earn a few trips so she can research the area."

Nina clapped. "I do think I love you, Adam. That's a fabulous idea. I know I'd read that article. There have been several times I've ventured to new countries and felt terribly ill-matched to the population. Sometimes looking like a tourist makes you a target for ruffians."

Kano's mouth lifted in one corner. "Adam does tend to come up with some of my best ideas. I see no reason we couldn't give it a whirl."

"That was very kind, Adam, dear," Judith said, taking Adam by surprise. "We've been trying to convince Kano to do more to support Nina's dreams for years. He never listens to us."

"Oh, do be quiet," Nina fussed before Adam had time to get upset. "Kano has offered me work in the past, but I have no interest in moving across the pond. All my friends are here."

Adam eyed her dark hair and gorgeous features, wondering why she wasn't married. She had to be close to thirty, but Kano hadn't mentioned a man in connection with her name. He made a mental note to be nosy later.

"You know what I mean," Judith said, making Adam wonder if anyone ever knew what she meant other than she'd intended to be mean. "Ever since Gerald died, you've been listless and jetting around the world with no real purpose. You can't count on your brother forever. He's likely to drop us all at any time.'

"Thanks for that," Kano muttered.

Adam tried keeping up. "Who's Gerald?"

Nina gave his arm a pat. "My husband."

Seemed there'd be no need to pry later. "That's sad," Adam said for lack of anything more. He'd never been good at dealing with death.

"It's fine," Nina said with a kind smile. "It was several years back. Mum and Dad just have a hard time accepting I don't need a man to fulfill me. I'm happy with life as it is now."

"That's exactly why you'll never find anyone. It's like we're doomed to never have grandchildren."

Kano chuckled. "You never know. I could adopt."

Adam switched his gaze from person to person as they swapped jibes. He was coming to understand this was the norm for them. It was a nightmare for him, but they were obviously accustomed to this barely veiled hatred of one another. All

Adam wanted was to make it through the rest of the day with his skin intact.

*

The flat had three bedrooms but felt like a studio after exposing Adam to his family. He wanted to hide, but it seemed as if Adam was right on top of him inside the large apartment. The horror written on the man's face all the way through their meal said it all—Kano's family really was every bit as bad as he believed. Kano paced the room. He tried focusing on his surroundings. Since relocating to the US, he'd kept this flat, since he was here quite a bit throughout the year. Sometimes, he wondered if he should sell it and never return. Hell, perhaps he should set it ablaze to keep from changing his mind.

The sitting room was painted a dark shade of yellow. Personally, he hated it. Kano had let Nina decorate because he couldn't be bothered and it gave her something to do. In truth, she was the only reason he kept coming back. The years had soured her personality. At one time, she'd been the nicest person he knew. Years alone with their parents' disapproval had left her bitter. Kano couldn't judge. After one lunch, he was ready to lash out at any target.

Unfortunately, the only one in sight was Adam. He would not show that man his temper, especially considering the wary glint in Adam's eyes. For ten minutes, he'd watched Kano eat up the floor from his spot on the hard settee. Adam hadn't said a word, which was just as well, since anything he had to say would probably match Kano's already dark thoughts. Kano didn't know what he'd been thinking by bringing Adam along. Mostly, he'd been thinking he didn't want to be away from the man long enough to make this trip alone. Also, he'd hoped Adam would soften his family somehow. To him, it seemed impossible to hold on to an ounce of real anger in Adam's presence. Instead, Kano had exposed Adam to something ugly. He didn't know how to take it back.

"Are you okay?"

Adam's softly spoken question drew Kano up short. His gaze met Adam's. Kano couldn't look away. "Yes. No," he admitted as quickly. "Forget about me. How are you?"

"Worried about you." The truth in Adam's voice had Kano's shoulders dropping another inch beneath the weight of the day. "Tell me what you have going on inside your head."

He couldn't. Kano had already exposed the man to too much ugliness in one day. "I haven't given you your present yet," he said instead.

The discomfort written on Adam's face

had Kano biting back a laugh. It should be illegal for anyone to be so innocent and sweet. "Um. No. You said you didn't want me to get you anything."

"That's you. I don't play fair."

Adam growled. Kano's heart melted at the adorable sound. "I'll have my revenge."

"I can't wait," Kano said, never meaning anything more in his life. "However, I took your reaction to me asking you what you wanted into consideration and I didn't get you a huge gift." It was only a small lie. The present itself wasn't huge. The price tag was, but Adam didn't need to know that.

Some of the wariness left Adam's eyes. "Okay. I guess I can deal with something small."

A roar of satisfaction ran through Kano. "Brilliant. Give me a second," he said, heading for his room. He found the small jewelry box he'd brought with him and returned to the sitting room. Kano held the box out to Adam. "The first time we met, I imagined you wearing something exactly like this as a nose ring. It would mean a great deal to me to see it now."

Adam flipped open the box. The tiny blue diamond twinkled. "Wow. This is gorgeous."

"It's a Blue Moon Diamond," Kano explained. "As soon as I saw it, I knew it belonged on you."

Adam stared down at the gift, robbing Kano from seeing his reaction. "It's beautiful," Adam said. His voice came out sounding low.

Just like you. Kano bit back the words as they raced to his tongue.

Adam's chin lifted. To Kano's surprise, the man's eyes swam with tears. "Thank you." Adam set the box aside and stood. Before Kano guessed at his intentions, Adam hugged him. Lust slammed into

Kano. He immediately readjusted his body, hoping Adam hadn't felt the way he'd gone hard. Adam didn't let go. Neither did Kano.

"Thank you for not running away screaming today," Kano said as he buried his nose in the crook of Adam's neck and inhaled. He wanted to hold the man forever.

"Running never occurred to me. Physically fighting someone did." Adam's confession pulled a chuckle from Kano. His next words had the sound dying on Kano's lips while stealing another piece of his heart. "You're amazing, and you deserve better. If they won't tell you how blessed they are to have you, I will. They're not the only ones. Meeting you was one of the greatest days of my life." Adam didn't give Kano time to respond before changing the subject. "When is your birthday?"

"April first," Kano said, his voice giving

away how moved he was by Adam's praise.

Adam's laugh vibrated against Kano's skin. It was nice. He couldn't remember the last time anyone had simply held him.

"You're an April's Fool baby."

Kano lifted his head and met Adam's gaze. "I'm definitely a fool." He focused on Adam's mouth, as if punctuating his claim. Desire owned him. He craved Adam's kiss even though he didn't know the man's flavor. Without thought, Kano brushed his fingers across Adam's bottom lip. He felt Adam stop breathing. As if needing to prove he'd lost his senses, Kano shifted, his body going flush against Adam's. All wisdom fled. Adam was hard for him. There was no missing the erection pressed between them or the flush forming on Adam's cheeks. The man wanted him. Kano had hoped but never dared dream. Kano dipped his chin, intent on capturing the lips that had taunted him for months.

Adam stepped out of his hold, denying Kano. "Should I try it on and see how it looks?" he asked, picking up the box. Without waiting for an answer or looking back, Adam headed for the bathroom. Kano didn't breathe again until the door closed behind Adam. He didn't think he could take back that moment of holding Adam. They were Pandora's box. Everything was out there now. Kano had seen the lust in Adam's eyes, and if he knew nothing else about himself, Kano knew he wouldn't stop until Adam belonged to him. The problem was, Kano wasn't sure Adam didn't already own him.

Chapter 4

It was as if they never touched. Through late nights and long trips, Kano hadn't seen a glimmer of the desire Adam had shown him in London. The man was damn good at avoiding Kano's every advance. That was probably why Kano couldn't stop staring at Adam now, or any other time for that matter. Adam was smiling. Kano didn't think Adam was aware of the grin stretching his lips, but Kano clung to every changing nuance. Tim kept catching his eye and smirking. It was possible Kano hadn't done a great job of hiding his longing. In his defense, he'd never met anyone like Adam. He was certain he'd dated people who'd been fond of him in the past, but no one had ever cared about Kano as much as Adam did for no reason at all. The man showed his affection in everything he did.

Two hours earlier, Kano asked Adam to put together a how-to article on finding the perfect shade of lipstick for each person's complexion. This was what led to the smiling and Kano's inability to look away. Adam always had such amazing ideas for the magazine, so Kano had been trying to pass more responsibility the man's way. Adam had taken it in stride. Tonight, he knew he'd made the right decision. The smile Adam wore... damn. He couldn't stop staring at it.

"You look happy." Kano couldn't stop the words any more than he could stop the way he fell for Adam a little more every day.

Adam flashed Kano a grin that tightened his groin. "I am. This isn't what I expected I'd be doing when I moved here, but I still love it."

"What was your hope? I mean, what

did you dream you'd accomplish after your internship with Rylan?"

Adam's expression stoked a long dead fire inside Kano. He reminded Kano of how it felt to be young, have dreams, and the world of possibilities at his feet. The small smile touching Adam's lips also had Kano's mouth watering from the desire to taste him.

Adam shrugged. "I wanted something huge— like head artist of a Broadway show. Maybe, eventually, my own makeup line." Adam chuckled, as if he thought he sounded ridiculous. "I'm not sure really. Maybe I wanted the whole world to be my masterpiece?"

Instead of commenting on Adam's confession and risking saying the wrong thing, Kano latched on to a different detail in Adam's story. "Do you like the theatre?"

Adam's eyes shone bright with

happiness as he answered. "Yes. I've been to several shows back home. It's probably nothing compared to what they have here, but I still loved it."

"I have tickets to tonight's Broadway event. Since I don't care to go alone, I didn't intend to go at all, but I'd be willing to reconsider if you'd go with me."

For a full minute, Adam eyed him in silence. "Are you asking me on a date?"

In the name of fairness, Kano didn't want any misunderstandings. "Yes."

"Does my job depend on my answer?" Adam asked, not pulling any punches.

"No."

"Then no," Adam said, not hesitating to shut Kano down.

Despite Adam's quick rejection, a smile exploded across Kano's face. "What if I'd said yes?"

"The answer still would've been no."

Rather than dissuading Kano, Adam's

89

response heightened Kano's interest. No doubt Adam came from a nice family that would welcome him home with open arms, but if Kano put him out, the man's career was dead. In spite of that knowledge, Adam refused to be bullied. He was the sexiest and most confident man Kano had met in ages.

Adam stood and gathered his things. "I'll see you on Monday."

Before he made it to the door, Kano called out, stopping him. "At least let Tim drive you home. It's late."

Adam didn't turn or slow. "No, thank you. I'm a big boy."

The door slid closed behind him before Kano had time to respond. Kano headed for his coat. He caught sight of Tim smiling before the man had time to rearrange his features.

"You're enjoying this, aren't you?"

Tim snorted. "Immensely."

"I'll win him."

Always the loyal one, Tim nodded. "Without a doubt."

"What are your thoughts on the matter?" Kano asked, needing an outsider to tell him if he was only thinking with his dick. "Am I making a fool of myself?"

Tim shook his head. "No more than anyone who's fallen head over heels. You've met your match."

Kano dipped his chin, acknowledging Tim's words before heading for the door. "That's what I was afraid of."

*

Adam's heart didn't stop racing until he reached the end of the block. Kano had asked him on a date. How long could he keep resisting? He already went to bed each night thinking about that almost kiss. It had been a nice offer too. The man hadn't offered a run through a drive-thru and a hand job. It was a freaking

Broadway show. In high style, no doubt. They would've been seen by everyone who was anyone in the most public way possible... on a date. He'd asked in front of Tim too, as if he didn't care at all what people thought. The idea had Adam back on the edge of hyperventilating.

To calm himself, Adam slowed his pace and dug through his pocket. He came out with a Taser Tyler had given him the night before he'd left for New York. After switching off the safety and tightening his grip, Adam picked up his pace once more. Tyler had done Adam a huge favor. He'd given Adam peace of mind. Sometimes this place got the best of him. Everything looked like a trap waiting to swallow him whole. Most likely, no one even noticed him. He was just another face in the crowd. Kano had left him feeling raw and exposed.

"Adam, hold up."

At the sound of Kano's thick British accent, Adam's eyes fell closed. He wasn't sure how much more temptation he could withstand tonight. Still, he slowed. It was as if his feet had a mind of their own. They knew Adam secretly craved every second of Kano's company. He glanced over as Kano reached his side. His face was flushed from the cold, making his light-colored eyes seem all that much brighter.

"If you won't let Tim take you home, at least let me walk you there," Kano said the moment he caught up with Adam.

"I'm out of your way," Adam said instead of answering.

"You're never out of my way."

Jesus. How was he supposed to resist? "Okay." Adam heard himself accept as if his answer came from a stranger's lips. He resumed his pace. Kano fell into step beside him.

"What do you do for fun?" Kano asked

after barely a minute passed. "It's Friday night and you've turned down a nice offer for the evening. You're on your way home, and I've never heard you speak of anything other than work. What do you do when you're not with me?"

Think about being with you. The traitorous thought passed through his head, forcing Adam to clench his teeth to keep from saying the words. Instead, he offered a different embarrassing truth. "Nothing. I don't know anyone here, and— truthfully—I'm not here to make friends. Right now, I'm all about carving my path in life."

"Your path sounds lonely."

At Kano's quietly spoken observation, Adam's chest tightened. The need to deflect rose up and choked him. In response, his voice came out overly bright as he called out, "What about you, Tim? You're always around. What do you do to unwind?"

"Tim went home."

Adam glanced behind them at Kano's announcement. Tim wasn't there. "Huh. I don't know if I've ever seen you without him in public. I was certain he would be right on our heels. Who'll keep you from getting mobbed?"

Kano motioned at the crowd of people walking in every direction around them. "Look around. Out here, at night, and in the cold, everyone looks the same. Their heads are down and their pace is faster than usual. Everyone has somewhere to be. Someplace warmer. No one is worried about who I am."

Kano was right. No one looked at anyone here, or spoke, or apologized for stepping on you. Where he was from, people held the door for the person behind them, asked strangers about their day, and said thank you. Sometimes, Adam felt like he'd moved to a different planet. Rather than sulk, as he wanted to do, Adam pressed on. He focused on the gorgeous man walking beside him.

"What about you? You're always on the go. Are you like that when you're not working or do you lounge around in silk pajamas while eating expensive chocolate?" Adam laughed at his ridiculous question even as he asked it.

"I wouldn't know," Kano answered, sounding sad. "There's never a moment when I'm not working. *Today's Beauty* is me and I'm it. This is my life's blood. My dream. I eat, drink, and sleep this magazine. One day, I woke up filled with so much passion I couldn't function unless I was working toward achieving my dream. Then, it took over everything."

There was so much fervor in Kano's voice, Adam couldn't stop staring at him. He made Adam want to help him hang on to whatever drove him, and join him on the adventure. Kano made owning *Today's Beauty* sound like a trip to the moon where they'd experience things no other man had achieved. Adam couldn't explain Kano's effect on him. He just made Adam long for everything and believe he could have it. Being in Kano's company was exhilarating.

Kano glanced over. His expression transformed. He winced. "Sorry. I get carried away."

Adam shook his head. "Don't apologize. My uncle, Jace. He raised me," Adam explained. "He's always fed my dreams. No matter how out of reach I thought my goals were, he stood behind me and urged me to believe I could be anything. So, yeah, I'm driven too, because I want to show him he was right to believe in me. Being here, away from his positive influence, I've wilted a bit," Adam admitted, feeling like a failure for a moment. "But your enthusiasm is catching. I like listening to you talk about the magazine. It feeds my drive." In truth, he could listen to Kano talk about the lifespan of bugs around the world. It didn't matter what the man said. Adam just wanted to soak up his energy and *be* with him.

"You were raised by your uncle? Where are your parents?" Kano asked the question as if he'd never heard of anyone not having parents. His confusion had Adam biting back a chuckle in spite of the heavy topic.

"They were killed in a car accident when I was twelve. I'm thankful I had them for as long as I did. They were amazing parents."

"I'm sorry to hear they're gone, but I'm glad you ended up with someone who did right by you. In a way, I feel like a total shit for not knowing this already. When you've said you're going home to your family for the weekend, or whatever, I've always assumed you meant parents. Since you've never expounded, I thought maybe you weren't close, which—as you know—is a sentiment I fully understand. You say you uncle's name is Jace? What's he like? Now I must know everything."

Adam monopolized the conversation for the remainder of their walk. He told Kano all about not speaking for three years and Jace's unwavering support. Adam went on to tell Kano of Jace's recent marriage and subsequent decision to walk away from everything to spend time with his new husband. He couldn't blame Jace. Jace had been the adult for years, never enjoying anything for himself. Everything was always for everyone else. Adam loved Jace had made this decision to be selfish for a while. By the time Adam was telling

Kano about Jace catching a shark while fishing in Australia, they'd reached his apartment. He blinked, wondering how long he'd stood with his back leaned against his door and telling his ass. Adam blushed. "I guess I miss him more than I realized."

Kano didn't look the least bit bored. His smile said he'd be willing to stand there all night. "I could take you to see him. We could fly out tomorrow and be back before my first appointment on Monday. Nothing and no one is that far away when you have a private plane at your disposal."

The discomfort was back. Adam was staring at a man who was out of his league again. It was funny how Kano could make him forget. "It's okay. I'll find a way to visit him soon."

Kano took a step forward. Adam pressed closer to the door. He couldn't breathe. He was trapped. "No one would know you'd accepted my offer. You don't have to worry people would judge you. I'm offering as a friend, not your boss."

"You're always my boss," Adam said, feeling moved to point out the obvious. "I don't want to be the cliché former intern turned love affair."

Kano's eyes flashed with humor. "Is that what you have in your head?" Kano shifted even closer as he added, "You think too much." His hands flattened against the door on either side of Adam, boxing him in. Adam swallowed a burble of hysterical laughter. Right now, he couldn't think at all. Kano smelled like the billions he was worth. Heat poured from his skin, warming Adam. Everything about the man was too much. "For once, tell your brain to bugger off," Kano whispered. His head lowered. Adam panicked. He hit Kano with the Taser. If the man looked stupid while getting hit with a huge dose of electricity, Adam didn't wait around to find out. He zapped Kano fast and leapt inside his apartment before slamming the door in his face.

Adam tossed the Taser to the floor as if it had betrayed him. His chest heaved like he'd ran for miles as he clung to the slab of wood separating him from Kano. What the fuck had he done? No doubt he was fired now. Was Kano okay? What if he'd stopped the man's heart? For all he knew, Kano was sprawled out in the hallway dead. Fuck him sideways. He'd been so focused on not letting Kano get under his skin, he'd turned into a goddamn idiot. Before he could chicken out, Adam threw open the door.

Kano's sexy as sin eyes were narrowed and murder stared at Adam. He took a step forward. Adam took one back. Before he knew what was happening, Kano's mouth covered his and the door slammed closed behind him. The man's kiss was everything Adam feared it would be. It was all-consuming and dripped with sexual promise. Everything powerful about Kano existed in the stroke of his tongue. His kiss was as confident as the man. Adam tore his mouth away, hoping to still save himself. Kano didn't retreat. His mouth moved from Adam's lips to his jaw before finding his ear. He bit Adam's lobe.

"You fucking tazed me."

Adam had nothing. He had done that.

Kano shoved Adam's coat down his arms, trapping him inside the material. "Was it worth it?" he asked as he bit the side of Adam's neck. "You've taunted me with this gorgeous body for months. Still, I would've left you at the door unmolested. Now, I'm not feeling especially nice."

What could Adam say? If roles were reversed, he'd probably be out for blood.

Not to mention, his dick beat against his zipper, begging Kano to touch it.

Kano pushed the coat to the floor and peeled off his as well before reclaiming Adam's mouth. With his arms free, Adam realized he'd yet to touch Kano. Even while held captive in a lust-fueled haze, he couldn't let himself go.

*

Kano lifted his head and glanced around, searching for a place to continue this. His gaze landed on the couch. He headed for it, pulling Adam along in his wake. After planting his ass on the sofa, he urged Adam to straddle his hips before recapturing the man's mouth. Adam kissed like a man starved for human contact. Kano would know. He didn't make time for dating. Most of the time, he didn't miss having someone to savor. Adam was the exception to everything, it seemed. He couldn't get enough of the sexy makeup artist. Kano liked having him around. He just liked Adam. Not so much at the moment. However, right now, he wanted to fuck Adam hard and punish him. The guy was still amazing, though.

Kano had to pull away as a bout of laughter sneaked out. "You're a complete nutter."

Adam blushed bright red.

A sigh escaped Kano as he leaned his head back against the couch and eyed Adam as he massaged the man's thighs. "What am I supposed to do with you now?"

Adam gnawed on his bottom lip as if it held his guilt. In truth, Kano had never seen anyone look more riddled with that particular emotion. "Does it hurt?"

Instead of answering, Kano chose to exploit the moment. "I think you should kiss it and make it better."

Adam's gaze slid down Kano's body. "I panicked. Honestly, I'm not sure where I got you."

Lust clawed at Kano's insides, making it hard for him to concentrate. "Upper thigh."

Adam glanced down, looking horrified. He tried scrambling from Kano's lap, but Kano wouldn't let him. "Oh, my god. You've got me sitting right where I hurt you."

"I'm a lot harder than I look," Kano said, intentionally choosing that verbiage.

Adam's cheeks pinkened again.

This man was way too innocent to be alone with Kano. Kano would eat him alive. Sometimes, being a gentleman sucked. Kano sighed. "Kiss me again, and I'll leave you be for the night. With all forgiven."

Adam moved slowly. There was nothing practiced about his seduction. Kano was still seduced in every way. By the time Adam's lips touched Kano's in an innocent kiss, Kano's breath stuttered from his lungs from the impact on his senses. Then Adam's tongue touched the corner of Kano's mouth. The muscles in Kano's chest twitched as he held himself in check.

"Tell me to honor my word," Kano said between kisses. For his cock's sake, he prayed Adam wouldn't toss him out.

Adam slipped to the floor between Kano's thighs. Kano held his breath. He'd fantasized about Adam in just this position a million times.

"Where did I get you?"

Kano silently tapped the spot on his upper right thigh where Adam had hit him with God only knows how many volts.

While holding Kano's stare, Adam dipped his head and touched his lips to the spot. The kiss was a light one. Kano felt it like the lash of a whip. No doubt a wet spot was forming at the front of his underwear from his dick leaking.

Adam's lips lingered. Kano stared down at his bowed head, fighting his nature.

"Tell me to go," Kano demanded, sounding husky and turned on.

Adam lifted his head.

Kano almost came. A flush rode high on the man's cheeks and his eyes were slightly unfocused. He'd never seen anyone look more aroused.

"Ask me to stay," Kano whispered.

Adam held his stare. Kano held his breath. A series of musical chimes broke the spell. Adam stood and pulled his phone from his back pocket, making Kano realize the man's phone was ringing. Adam glanced at the face of the device. "It's Jace. If I don't answer, he'll worry."

Kano moved to stand. He was disappointed but prepared to show himself out. Adam answered the call while pressing his hand against Kano's chest, stopping him from leaving. Kano relaxed his spine against the couch once more. He stared at Adam's face even though Adam's gaze moved everywhere but in Kano's direction.

"Hello?" Adam said as he put the phone on speaker and set it on the couch next to Kano.

"Hey, you're on speaker," a man who must be Jace said.

"You too," Adam said with a chuckle as he went back down onto his knees. "Does that mean Uncle Tyler is hanging around in the background?"

"I'm here," a second male voice said. "Have you had to use that Taser on any strange dudes yet?" Tyler asked, his voice laced heavily with laughter.

Kano smiled.

Adam laughed. He moved between

Kano's knees and loosened Kano's tie. Kano's smile slipped away, replaced with hunger. "No strange dudes, no," Adam said. He kept his gaze locked on his task as he slipped the buttons loose on Kano's shirt. Kano held his breath. Everything else became background noise as his heartbeat pulsed in his ears.

"We were calling because we have our itinerary for our next three months of travel. I wanted to go over it with you, and see if our travel plans put us anywhere near where you'll be. If so, maybe your boss will give you an afternoon off to spend with us."

Adam paused and met Kano's stare. His eyebrows rose in question. Kano nodded, letting Adam know that could be arranged.

"I'm sure Kano wouldn't mind giving me a couple of hours to see you."

"Awesome," Jace said, sounding

happy. "I keep meaning to tell you, Kano is an amazing name. It sounds foreign. Where is he from?"

Adam's gaze stayed locked on his hands as he moved to Kano's belt. He silently slid the leather loose. "Weybridge. It's near London."

Jace let out a low whistle. "Aren't there a ton of millionaires there?"

The front of Kano's pants opened beneath Adam's fingers. "I have no idea, but I wouldn't be surprised."

Kano couldn't believe Adam held up his end of the conversation while he was killing him. Drawing a slow breath through his nose, Kano prayed he wouldn't explode the moment Adam touched his cock. He'd never wanted anyone as badly for so long. Jace rattled off a set of dates and places. Kano tried listening. After all, if there was any chance of meeting Adam's family, Kano wanted it. He craved having all of Adam, like a sickness. It was impossible to listen to Jace while Adam handled his dick. With Kano's erection free, Adam dipped his head and licked Kano from root to crown. A gasp escaped him. Kano slapped a hand over his mouth to keep from making another noise.

"Are you doing anything tonight for Valentine's Day?"

Adam sat back on his heels and focused on the phone. He blinked, looking confused. He glanced Kano's way and mouthed, "It's Valentine's Day?"

Kano nodded.

Adam focused on the phone once more. "It's Valentine's Day?" He sounded every bit as confused as he looked.

Jace growled. "I'm not surprised you didn't know. Look, I know you have big dreams and I want all those things for you, but I also don't want you to wake up one day and realize none of it means a thing because you're alone."

"I don't feel the least bit alone," Adam said, flashing Kano a conspiratorial smile before going down on him and damn near making Kano swallow his tongue.

Silence rang through the line, or maybe Kano had lost his ability to hear. Kano's ass left the couch. The way Adam's hot mouth sucked his dick was the most amazing sensation on the planet. His fingers found Adam's hair.

"We could come see you before we set out for London."

Adam pulled away for a second. "That's not necessary, Jace. We'll be in London too next week."

Would they? Kano couldn't think, especially since Adam went right back to allowing Kano to fuck his willing mouth. This wasn't at all how Kano pictured spending his night. This was torture.

Moans kept rising in his throat. Kano had to swallow them to keep from giving Adam away. He hadn't had to hide his pleasure in years. Adam tugged on Kano's pants, dragging them farther down even as he kept the perfect pace, threatening to steal Kano's orgasm. He didn't know if he could hold on to his silence while he came. He loved the way Adam's mouth felt too much.

"That's fantastic. I had my hopes up we would see you soon, but that's even sooner than I dreamed. Yay. I'm so excited."

"He's missed you a little," Tyler said, reminding Kano there were two men unknowingly listening to him get his dick sucked. A burble of laughter rose in his throat. Kano bit his bottom lip—hard— trying to keep the noise from escaping.

Adam's eyes flipped up, meeting Kano's gaze. The sight of his wet cock slipping from Adam's lips while the man boldly held his stare would've sent Kano over the edge if Adam hadn't chosen that moment to pull away.

"I miss you too. Let me talk to Kano," Adam said while lightly stroking Kano's erection. "Once he tells me his schedule, I can give you an exact time. Okay?"

"That's fine. Just text me. I guess we'll let you go. We have a date night planned."

"Okay," Adam said. His gaze never wavered from Kano. "I love you." The breath caught at the back of Kano's throat. If he didn't know better, he would've sworn Adam's words were meant for him. Hunger like he'd never known before consumed him. He wanted Adam's love.

"Love you too," both men said before the line went silent and the face of Adam's phone went black.

"You have amazing restraint," Adam

said before taking Kano's cock between his lips once more. Kano wasn't sure if that was true. In his defense, his brain couldn't function with all his blood racing to his dick. With no one listening, a low moan escaped Kano as Adam sucked hard. He couldn't stop running his hands through Adam's hair, touching the man every place he could reach. Adam's tongue lapped at Kano's crown, teasing the oversensitive nerve endings. Kano scratched at the couch cushions, trying to find purchase. The pressure became too much. His explosion rocked him. Kano couldn't keep his eyes open. His dreams coming true was too much for him.

Without a real plan, he pushed and shoved until he had Adam on his back on the floor. He straddled the man's hips and captured Adam's mouth, the flavor of his cum mixed with Adam's unique taste stealing his every thought. All he could think about was how much he loved this man. Those three words became a mantra in his head to the point Kano wasn't sure he wasn't chanting them. For months, Adam had been such a huge part of his life. Now, Kano couldn't imagine going a day without him. Holding Adam. Kissing him. It was everything.

Adam shook. Kano didn't know if it was from fear or desire, but he couldn't stop touching the man. His lips moved from Adam's mouth to his throat. "So amazing," Kano praised against the man's skin as he moved lower. He used his teeth to move Adam's shirt higher, freeing him to lick Adam's stomach. His fingers worked the man's jeans loose. A breath he hadn't known he'd been holding came out on a *whoosh* when Adam's erection finally filled his palm. "Jesus, Adam. All I want to do anymore is be with you."

Somewhere inside Kano's jacket, his

phone rang.

"Bloody hell. Are you fucking kidding me? It's Tim's ringtone. I can't ignore it."

Adam nodded, but his eyes looked a bit crazed. "Yeah. I know."

After snagging the corner of his jacket, Kano dragged it closer and dug out his phone. He swiped his hand over his face, hoping he didn't sound as breathless as he felt.

"What?" he barked, uncaring if he sounded rude. His tone was nothing compared to how he felt.

"Sorry to bother you, Kano. The alarm company just called. Someone tried to break into the building. The police have asked for you to meet them."

Kano's rage over the interruption was deep. "Goddamn it. Why won't they let you take care of it?"

"Don't know," Tim said, sounding nowhere near as contrite as he should.

"They said it had to be you."

"Fucking hell. I'm at Adam's. Pick me up."

"Okay. Give me ten minutes."

Kano didn't want to say anything to disrespect Adam, but he also wasn't through with him. "Don't rush."

"Oh," Tim said, sounding as if he'd finally caught on. "You got it."

Kano hung up without saying goodbye. He met Adam's stare. Disappointment ate ten years from Kano's life. "Someone tried to break into the building. I have to meet with the police."

"Right now?" Adam sounded every bit as desperate as Kano felt.

He rushed to reassure him. "Don't worry. I have no intention of leaving you like this. I don't care if they have to wait. You wait for no one," Kano said, hearing the growl in his voice, incapable of hiding it. Adam came before everything and

119

everyone. Since he was short on time, Kano didn't play. After tossing his phone aside, he slipped down Adam's body and took the man to the back of his throat. The sound coming from Adam had Kano's dick stirring once more. There was no mercy in Kano's heart. He refused to leave Adam hanging while he dealt with business. That meant setting a pace guaranteeing quick results. This wasn't how Kano imagined his first sexual encounter with Adam, but he would take whatever he could get.

His throat burned as he swallowed Adam's cock. He didn't stop. Kano did it over and over, using the man's moans as his guide. The way Adam's hips left the floor and his fingers dug into the back of Kano's neck, said a lot about his level of pleasure.

"Kano, please?" Adam begged.

Kano's eyes stung. He'd never willingly

make Adam beg for anything, but hearing the man plead for release was the most addictive experience. Saliva ran down his fingers as Kano pumped the man's cock while hollowing out his cheeks and sucking at the perfect pace. He felt Adam's muscles tense. Kano doubled his efforts. He wanted Adam's cum filling his mouth. When it happened, Adam cried his name. A feeling of completeness overcame Kano. No one could tell him he hadn't been meant to meet Adam. They fit. When he hadn't been paying attention, Kano had met the man of his dreams. Even the flavor of Adam's cum was delicious. Kano knew he'd have to stop himself from trying to taste it every day.

Kano turned his head and wiped his face on Adam's stomach. "I don't want to leave." Even to him, the admission came out sounding fierce.

Adam massaged his scalp. "In a few

minutes, you'll come down from your high and you'll be furious someone tried to break into your building." Adam's claim came out sounding breathless. "But I hope when you get there, you'll still be half hard and thinking about me."

With a chuckle, Kano climbed up Adam's body. "That's true every second of every day," Kano admitted before touching his lips to Adam's. The way Adam's tongue lightly traced Kano's bottom lip was so damn sweet, it stole Kano's heart. He let it go on for longer than necessary before forcing Adam to deepen their kiss. Adam moaned. The sound vibrated around their entwined tongues. "Adam," Kano whispered into the man's mouth. "I don't want to go."

Adam's arms tightened around him. "London next week," Adam reminded him.

"We won't be alone." It was true. They were never alone. Tim was always there.

Kano needed him and genuinely liked the man, but right now, firing Tim looked like a good option. If not for Tim's constant presence, they might have been doing this much sooner.

"That's true." Adam's tone kept his feelings hidden on the matter. "But I like knowing Tim is there to keep you safe. If anything happened to you, I think it would kill me."

Kano pressed his forehead to Adam's. It wasn't an admission of love, but Kano would take it. Adam cared. This wasn't some heat of the moment occurrence. The phone rang again. A heartfelt sigh escaped Kano. "That would be Tim, letting me know he's here."

"I imagine so," Adam agreed. "Text me and let me know how it goes."

"Okay."

"Also, let me know when you make it home safely."

Kano's body shook with barely suppressed laughter. He couldn't help it. Happiness was choking him. "You got it."

"Kiss me one more time and then answer your phone before Tim beats down my door."

Greed overcame Kano. He wanted more than one kiss. It was on the tip of his tongue to beg Adam to give him forever. As their lips met, Kano made Adam a thousand silent promises. He would see the man's every dream come true, even if it killed him.

Chapter 5

Adam played on his phone, ignoring Kano. It had Kano's skin crawling. He wanted to shake Adam. Make him acknowledge the change in their relationship. Going by the way Adam had acted around him since Valentine's, anyone would think nothing happened at all. Kano fucking despised it. It was as if he meant nothing. Two hours in to their flight to London, Tim had kicked back and passed out. A half hour passed, and still Kano spoke softly, hoping he could avoid waking Tim. He hoped to keep their conversation private.

"Have you solidified plans to meet Jace?"

Adam glanced his way. His beautiful eyes shone with happiness over the prospect of seeing the uncle he loved. "Yes. We're meeting for lunch tomorrow at The Village Port."

"I know the place. If you'd like, I could take you so you don't get lost. It's easier than you think to get turned around in London."

"No, thank you. I'll be fine."

Kano ground his back teeth. Adam wasn't fooling him. The man didn't want his uncles to meet Kano. For a good five minutes, Kano tried letting it go. He couldn't. "Is there a reason you don't wish me to meet Jace?"

Adam glanced away. Guilt etched his every line. He focused on Tim, as if ensuring the man really slept. Kano couldn't take any more. He stood and headed for the bathroom. After pulling the door open, he waved Adam inside.

"Please, step into my office."

Adam didn't immediately budge. "Are you asking or is my boss ordering me?"

A growl rose in Kano's throat and showed in his voice. "I don't give a shit what you have to tell yourself as long as you move your arse."

While looking wary and making Kano feel like shit, Adam slipped inside the tiny bathroom. Kano squeezed in too, before locking them inside.

He focused on Adam. "All right. We're alone. Spill."

Adam shrugged, but his eyes were sad. "People don't introduce their bosses to their family unless they're saying there's more to their relationship than business."

"There is more to our relationship than business," Kano said without missing a beat and sounding as if he thought Adam's statement was as idiotic as it was.

Adam stared at some point over Kano's shoulder, refusing to meet Kano's gaze. With each passing minute, Kano's temper rose. "I'm not sure what we are, Kano, but I know it wouldn't be right for you to meet my family. That's exactly why I haven't spoken to you about them before the other night. It just isn't right."

Before he realized it would happen, Kano pressed his weight into Adam, forcing the man to meet his stare.

"It wouldn't be right for me to do this either, but I am," Kano said, capturing Adam's mouth. Adam melted into his touch. His surrender didn't cool Kano's rage. Kano sucked Adam's bottom lip, sinking his teeth into the plump flesh before moving to Adam's jaw. He spoke against the man's skin. "It's improper for me to do this," he said, unbuttoning Adam's jeans and shoving his hand inside. Adam hardened against Kano's palm. "But I don't plan to stop." Kano sat down on the closed toilet and freed Adam's erection. "I damn sure shouldn't do this, but I am," Kano said, taking the man's cock between his lips. The last sight Kano had before closing his eyes and swallowing Adam's dick was Adam's knuckles whitening as he held on to the sink for support.

Kano didn't hold back. Every skill he'd perfected and all his anger went into blowing Adam. This man made him crazy, and not always in a good way. Each time he thought he made headway, Adam found a new way to put space between them. He honestly didn't believe Adam was playing hard to get. Kano didn't know what the fuck was going on. All he knew was, he fell a little more in love with Adam every day while Adam added another brick to his wall.

Harsh breaths and gasps filled the tiny bathroom. Adam's hips moved, fucking Kano's mouth. Still, he didn't touch Kano. Kano hated it. He pulled away, ignoring Adam's cry of protest, and focused on Adam.

"Fucking touch me, Adam. Quit stealing your affection from me." He hated himself in that moment. He despised the begging note to his voice. Kano stood and prepared to walk away and leave Adam hanging. He didn't care. Kano was exhausted with trying to pull some emotion from Adam, and questioning everything.

Adam reached out, stopping him. He pulled Kano in for a kiss. "I'm sorry," he whispered against Kano's lips before deepening their kiss. Adam caressed every place he could reach. He massaged Kano's erection through his pants. But that wasn't what melted Kano's heart. It was Adam's whispered confessions between kisses that softened Kano's temper, wiping it away. "You're amazing. I'm not ashamed of us. I'm just not ready, okay? Let me get used to this change between us before you meet Jace, please? Dang, I love the way you smell—like expensive spice." He sucked Kano's tongue. "The way you taste is even better—like champagne and chocolate covered strawberries."

Kano dipped lower and nipped at Adam's throat. "I don't need to meet your family right this second. Just don't shut me out, okay? Don't pretend this isn't happening."

Without waiting for Adam's agreement, Kano sat down and swallowed the man's cock once more, because he loved the way Adam tasted too.

"I'm more than aware this is happening," Adam said, sounding turned on. "Dang, Kano. I can't walk out of this bathroom covered in cum."

"Not a drop will touch your skin," Kano swore and he meant it. He wouldn't give up a trace of Adam. Kano wanted it all for himself.

Kano stroked Adam's dick while watching the man's face. He loved the arousal etching his features. Adam chewed his bottom lip before admitting, "I don't think I can make the same promise."

An unnamed pressure settled into the center of Kano's chest. Sometimes Adam's innocence was too much. "This isn't about reciprocation. Hell, this isn't even about sex. This is about my need to make you happy."

"I want to make you happy too," Adam whispered.

Kano's gaze dropped to where Adam's cock filled his hand. For a moment, he was mesmerized by the sight. The confession escaped as Kano dipped his head, needing to taste Adam. "I'm already ecstatic, because you're mine."

*

No one gave better hugs than Jace. Adam was a little biased, but he stood by his opinion. It was probably because Jace had always made him feel protected. Adam equally acknowledged it could be his massive muscles combined with how gentle he was. No matter what made it true, Adam held on for longer than necessary. It had only been about two and a half months since he last saw his uncle, but he'd never gone so long.

"We half expected this Kano guy to be with you," Tyler said as he got in on the hugging action.

Adam pasted on a fake smile and chose a seat. "What made you think that?"

Jace pulled out a chair across from him and sat. "You're here together. We would've liked to have met him."

"He's a busy man," Adam said, only half lying. "Besides, he knows how much I've been missing you. He wouldn't intrude."

"Huh," Tyler grunted.

"Yep," Jace said.

Adam glanced between the two, taking

in their matching knowing expressions while mulling over the conversation they were having that only they seemed to understand. A bad feeling churned in his gut. "What's that supposed to mean?"

They opened their menus and looked away. Jace was the one who answered. "Nothing. Kano owns *Today's Beauty*, right? That must make him at least our age."

Adam could play this game too. He opened his menu and focused on the small writing inside. "You'll have to narrow it down. There's almost ten years difference between you." Even Adam couldn't believe how bland he sounded.

Tyler chuckled, but Jace didn't let it go. "I'm thirty-four and Tyler is forty-three. Is he closer to me or Tyler?" He paused for a second before adding, "Or neither?"

Adam shrugged, acting as if he'd never considered Kano's age. "He closer to you than Tyler, I suppose."

"Wow," Tyler said, joining the conversation. "I expected someone as accomplished as him to be much older. Of course, I'm not sure if that's a good thing or not."

That got Adam's attention. "What's that supposed to mean?"

It was Tyler's turn to shrug. "You two spend a lot of time together, traveling, late nights..."

He obviously expected Adam to confess. It wasn't happening. Not yet. Maybe not ever. He wasn't sure where he stood with Kano. Possibly he was a passing fancy. Convenient. "I'm his personal stylist. He does a lot of TV interviews, magazine shoots, and fashion shows all over the world. Kano is the face of trend. Of course we spend a lot of time together. That's my job."

"I'd feel better if you'd let us meet the

guy."

An exasperated-sounding sigh escaped Adam. "He's my boss. Do you intend to interrogate every boss I have in my life? Plus, don't tell me Tyler hasn't already had him investigated, because I'm sure he has."

"So?" Tyler didn't look the least bit guilty at his admission. "You're leaving the country with some strange dude. Jace should know if he's a weirdo."

"He's not a weirdo," Adam said, barely stopping himself from slapping the table in his frustration.

"What is he then?" Jace asked, looking as if he might start yelling at any moment.

The confession slipped from Adam without thought. "He's amazing."

Tyler and Jace both had Cheshire smiles pop into place. Adam ground his back teeth. He'd been played. It was too late. The words were already in his throat.

"He's talented and kind. You have no idea how many times he's offered to fly me to Tennessee just because he knew I was homesick. Kano is a good man. You have nothing to worry about."

"Does this good man know you're in love with him?" Jace asked, going back to staring at the menu.

On a huff, Adam flipped up the menu and concentrated on figuring out what he wanted to eat. It all sounded disgusting. "If there's a God in Heaven, Kano doesn't have a clue." This time, he didn't bother checking their reactions. Jace knew Adam too well for him to ever lie anyhow.

* * *

By the time Adam made it back to the flat, after his visit with Jace, Kano was ready to climb the walls from boredom. The instant Adam came through the door, Kano's black mood fell away.

"Tim tells me he's staying at a hotel, and..." Adam's words died away as his gaze landed on the lit candles and wine. "What's all this?"

"You are de-stressing, and I'm babying you."

"But you always baby me," Adam said as Kano led him to the couch. He handed Adam a glass of wine. Adam sniffed it. "I don't like wine."

"You'll like this."

Adam's nose curled in the most adorable way. "That's what everyone says when they hand you a nasty glass of wine." He took a sip. "Okay, that's not horrible."

With a laugh, Kano held out a bottle of water to Adam. He'd known Adam would hate the alcohol. This was the tenth time Kano had tried turning Adam on to drinking without luck.

Adam flashed him a grateful smile and

set to washing the taste out of his mouth. "What have you been doing while I was away?" Adam asked as Kano settled in close. Adam immediately turned sideways and threw his legs across Kano's lap and snuggled in as close as possible. Kano loved these moments. With Adam waiting expectantly, Kano set to telling him all about his boredom and finally sending Tim away with orders to get Adam and then go enjoy himself. There was no sense in Tim being stuck watching Kano climb the walls.

"What's got you so antsy?" Adam's southern accent thickened as he asked the question.

Kano couldn't take it; he had to kiss Adam and find out if he could taste the way it sounded. He surged forward and captured Adam's lips.

Kano caught himself humming as Adam's tongue curled around his.

"Thinking about all this," Kano confessed as he changed angles. Kano pulled away before he ended up falling on Adam like a horny teenager when the man just got home. He toyed with Adam's hair as he put some distance between them, incapable of giving up touching the man completely.

"Tell me about your visit with Jace and Tyler."

Adam leaned into Kano's touch as he complied with Kano's demand. "I looked at lots of pictures of their travels. Oh, and did you know, they've decided to put Jace's house up for rent for at least the next year, so it won't sit empty and gives them a source of income while they're off doing their thing?"

"Sounds like a solid plan."

"It does," Adam agreed. "It's strange to see Jace so carefree. In a good way, of course. Double oh, why is the food so nasty here? I've never seen fish cooked so many ways and all of it is bad."

Against his will, Kano laughed. Adam's expression was too much. Kano had never seen anyone look so mortally offended by food. "We'll be back home tomorrow. I'll take you to get some real food first thing." Kano brushed his knuckles down Adam's jaw. "Until then, I suppose I'll have to keep you distracted from your hunger."

Silence fell between them as they stared at each other. The room had fallen dark as the sun set and at least one candle died away. Kano couldn't stop touching Adam. His fingertips traced the curve of Adam's cheek before caressing the man's bottom lip.

"I bet you've slept with thousands of men."

Adam's remark blindsided Kano. "Wow." Kano had not seen that one coming. He didn't even know where to start. First off, he was definitely insulted.

That was tops, but there was something vulnerable about Adam's words keeping Kano from flying into a rage. Instead, he swallowed down his ire and concentrated on Adam's needs. He hated the broken tone Adam used while making the claim. That hurt his heart. The man seemed to be under some delusions about Kano. Yes, Kano always got what he wanted. Money made life like that, but what Adam didn't understand was that was the exact reason Kano hadn't slept with thousands of men. Some people might be content with having someone simply because someone sexy wanted them, whether or not that person was truly interested in them as a person. He didn't want to fuck someone who pictured dollar signs while it happened. When Kano was inside someone, he needed them to see him. The real him—flaws and bad habits. His horrible temper. Kano's obsessive nature. He wanted someone who wanted him despite all those qualities.

"Would you believe me if I said that wasn't true?"

"Of course," Adam said without missing a beat. He meant it. Kano could see it in Adam's eyes. That was why he couldn't stay away from Adam.

"I don't sleep around."

"Oh," Adam said, not sounding anywhere near as relieved as Kano hoped. "Okay."

Adam chewed on his bottom lip. His eyes shone bright in the otherwise low-lit room. Kano couldn't look away. "Adam."

Adam immediately stopped worrying at his lip when Kano said his name. "Yes?"

"You can always ask me anything and I'll be honest with you."

"Okay."

Kano couldn't let this go, even with Adam's agreement. "You can also tell me anything. No judgments. Don't disappear inside your head. I do that a lot. Overthink things and make them bigger than they are."

"That's not what I'm doing."

Adam's admission came out sounding low. Kano matched his tone. "What are you doing, then?"

"Struggling with feeling inferior. It's a new thing for me."

The only thing saving Kano from flying into a rage was the fact that Adam had never said anything before now to show a lack of confidence. Wait. Adam really hadn't ever shown any weakness in anything he did. A horrible idea crept in. It couldn't be.

Kano cleared his throat. He didn't want to ask. He had to know. Like ripping off a bandage, he let the question fly. "Are you a virgin?" Even he winced at how crass the question sounded. Adam looked away. The silence following his inquiry was all the answer Kano needed. His shock was complete. It had never occurred to him. Adam was young, but he was a grown man. Then again, it seemed as if younger men were growing new morals. Not to mention, Adam was extremely career driven. It made sense he would set aside that part of himself to concentrate on making it in his profession.

Adam's continued silence crawled over Kano's skin. He hated he'd put Adam in this position. The man was amazing and his sex life didn't matter. Kano needed to fix it.

"Come here." The growled demand sounded even harsher than Kano intended. Adam let his legs fall to the floor and moved closer. "You're not allowed to be scared or embarrassed," Kano said before pressing a quick kiss to Adam's lips and coming to his feet. He knew his order

145

had been a ridiculous one, but he hated the idea of Adam fearing anything between them. He pulled Adam to his feet. With the man's hand held firmly in his, Kano headed for the bedroom. The way Adam silently obeyed said more about the man's level of nervousness than any amount of restless chatter would. He didn't bother turning on the lights. That was pressure Adam didn't need. At the edge of the bed, Kano urged Adam down onto the mattress before covering the man's body with his own. He kept his weight to one side and wasted no time tugging at the button of Adam's jeans.

"You've had my lips wrapped around your cock. Surely having my fist there won't break you."

Adam sucked in an audible breath before releasing a whimper at Kano's words.

He could feel Adam's heart racing.

146

Kano licked the man's bottom lip, doing his best to turn Adam's nervousness into lust. He didn't want to sleep apart again. If they didn't cross this line, Adam would keep putting more distance between them. Kano had been so focused on trying to break down the barrier of their different stations, he'd never considered there might be more to Adam's reluctance. He could make this man quiver. The muscles in Kano's stomach refused to relax. He'd known all along Adam was too innocent. That he would corrupt him. Now that the moment had arrived, something unexpected gnawed at Kano's brain. No one else had touched this sexy man. Adam was his in every way. Only his. It was humbling. At the same time, greed owned Kano. This was his man. He wouldn't let anything tear them apart.

Adam's fingertips skimmed Kano's back. Goosebumps rose beneath Adam's touch. Their tongues met and stroked. Kano dipped his hand inside Adam's pants. Pre-cum smeared his fingers as he encircled Adam's cock. He kept his touch light. Kano wasn't ready for Adam to come undone. His teeth sank into Adam's bottom lip and tugged. Sometimes he thought he could devour Adam. He could take over the man's existence. Sink into him.

"Tell me what you picture between us when you touch yourself."

A nervous-sounding chuckle left Adam. "Um. I don't know."

Kano stroked Adam's erection. The man wasn't anywhere near as aroused as he should be if he could still get embarrassed. "It's me, Adam. We're together. In the dark. No one will ever know anything you say to me." Kano intentionally kept his voice low and added deep kisses along with his promises. "All your fantasies can do is make me drip with need. Give me everything."

Adam's hands dove beneath the waistband of Kano's workout shorts and underwear. He massaged the globes of Kano's ass. "Sometimes you're on your knees." The admission came out sounding like a dirty secret, but Adam didn't stop. "Other times, you're in full Kano mode, being demanding and controlling. You make me hold your stare while you take me."

Kano took a deep breath. His body responded to Adam's words as if they were happening. He *was* the kind of man who would force Adam to keep his eyes open. Kano wanted Adam to see who owned him. While holding Adam's gaze, Kano dragged Adam's pants and underwear down his hips. Adam didn't protest.

"I don't want to hurt you, but I might."

Adam nodded. "It's okay. You look very

intense right now."

Kano tried to smile and failed. He felt intense. "I've been alone a long time," Kano heard himself admit. "Then you came along. I'm frightened of myself sometimes when it comes to you."

"Don't be afraid. I'm shaking inside enough for the both of us."

Adam's admission broke something loose inside Kano. He would take care of Adam. "I'm scared of you too."

Even in the dark, Kano didn't miss the way Adam's head cocked to one side in the man's curiosity. "Why?"

"Because you could break me, Adam. Like no one else on the planet, you could tear me down, leaving nothing but a smoldering pile of ash in your wake. No one else has ever had that kind of power over me." He didn't give Adam time to respond to his confession. "If I move away for a second, will you run?"

"No."

The sureness in Adam's voice had Kano's heart racing. For once, he believed Adam wouldn't get away. Leaning over the edge of the bed, he snagged his overnight bag. Kano dug around until he found a condom and a bottle of lube. He was back before Adam's body cooled. To be on the safe side, he captured Adam's mouth. He let Adam know with his touch they were just getting started. Kano kissed every place he could reach as he divested Adam of his clothing and tugged his away as well.

"From the first moment I saw you, I knew I'd met an angel," Kano confessed before opening his mouth over Adam's collarbone. In truth, Kano no longer knew what he said. It felt as if they were crossing an invisible line—like they were on the verge of becoming real. After popping the lid on the lube, Kano squirted a generous amount in his palm before fisting Adam's cock once more. Adam writhed beneath him. The sounds coming from the back of the man's throat drove Kano. His hand slipped lower. He massaged Adam's balls before moving between Adam's legs. For a minute, he simply used his lubed fingers to toy with Adam's asshole. Adam's fingers dug into his shoulders.

Kano had never made love to a virgin before. He had no idea what he was getting into. He'd never been more scared of hurting someone. Going slow, he dipped the tip of one finger inside, pushing past the ring of tight muscles. A low, deep moan vibrated from deep within Adam's chest. At the sound, Kano slipped a second finger inside. Adam was so tight. A fine sheen of sweat already coated Kano's skin at the thought of the man's heat squeezing his cock. While stretching the man's hole with his fingers, Kano probed with his dick, sliding inside a hair before immediately retreating. He realized he didn't have enough hands. The only way he could think to make this easier was Adam's orgasm.

"I need you to play with yourself, sweetheart."

Adam didn't hesitate to reach between them and palm his cock. The sweat on Kano's forehead increased. Between Adam's tight ass and the vision of him pumping his erection was killing Kano.

"Want you inside me," Adam begged, sounding breathless.

Kano held his breath and pushed deeper. Adam gasped. Kano froze. "I can stop," Kano said, sounding panicked even to his ears. It might cripple him for life, but he would stop if Adam asked.

Adam snagged the back of Kano's neck and pulled his head down, going nose to nose with him. "Kano, don't make me kill you," he said before lifting his head and closing the final gap between them. His kiss was fierce. Adam bit and sucked, as if trying to consume Kano. Adam's muscles tensed, as if bracing for an orgasm. Kano held his breath. Hot cum hit Kano in the chest. Adam's muscles relaxed, Kano surged forward, impaling Adam. A loud cry bounced off the walls of the room. Kano tried to hold still at the sound. Adam wasn't having it. With a shove and a flip, Kano found himself on his back with Adam straddling his hips. He rode Kano's dick as if he'd been craving it for years while Kano denied him. All Kano could do was try to keep pace. There was no holding back his orgasm. He'd wanted Adam for too long. The man's body felt too good. Pressure climbed up his cock before exploding into a blinding light. Kano gasped for air while chanting Adam's name, even as he tried kissing Adam at the same time. It was like coming down from a chemical high. His hands shook and his head felt like his brain hadn't had oxygen for five minutes. Every nerve ending tingled. He'd never been more aware of every surface his skin touched, especially where it met Adam's.

Their kiss went from deep and demanding to barely a brush of skin on skin. They clung. Harsh breaths fell between them. Adam closed his lips around Kano's bottom lip and held it there. Kano's fingers dug into his Adam's back, massaging as he tried to memorize every detail of the man. A mess of cum and sweat clung to their skin. Everything about the moment was fucking perfect.

"Kano," Adam whispered, capturing and holding Kano's full attention. "Thank you."

Kano ran his fingers through Adam's sweat-soaked hair, savoring every second.

"For what?"

"Not being angry because I didn't tell you."

With a roll, Kano had Adam tucked against his side. He found the man's gaze in the dark. He didn't know how to ease Adam's mind. Instead, he chose to go with his truth. "Thank you."

A low chuckle escaped Adam. "For what?"

"Not getting angry with me for continuously trying to steal something you weren't ready to give."

Adam pinched his side, pulling a surprised gasp from Kano. "I'm calling you lots of ugly names in my head right now." Adam rubbed the spot he'd pinched even as he made the claim.

Laughter started in Kano's stomach, making him shake before escaping his lips on a roar. He kissed Adam because he couldn't resist. "Good. I've always wanted

156

to be called Panthy Neveah Reighleigh Keeler." Adam's laughter joined his and vibrated through their kiss. Kano made a wish in that moment, tossing it out to any god listening. He prayed he could hang on to this amazing man forever. Kano couldn't go back to the humorless life he'd lived before Adam. It would kill him.

Chapter 6

It had taken Kano over a month for the truth to settle in. Adam didn't want anyone to know about them. At first, he'd thought Adam was too much of a professional to show affection at work. After almost six weeks of getting shut down during the day, Kano had come to accept what had his heart crying foul. Adam was ashamed. There were times when Kano didn't think about it. Then there were other times, when Adam's rejection was all Kano could think about. Times like today. It was only nine in the morning. The day hadn't truly begun, but Kano couldn't stop watching Adam and stewing. Each time Adam caught his eye, Kano held his breath as he searched for any of the affection Adam showed him last night. Instead, all Kano got was a bland smile before Adam looked away again.

By the third time, Kano couldn't take another second. "Tim, would you go and find Rylan? He has fifteen models waiting for him. The man is holding up an entire shoot with his tardy ways."

"On it," Tim said, coming to his feet.

As Tim headed for the door, Adam focused on Kano, looking concerned. "Should I go downstairs and fill in until Rylan gets here?"

"No. It's Rylan's responsibility. Plus, you're needed here."

Kano felt Adam's disappointment from across the room. That was another thing. Sometimes, Kano wondered if he was crushing Adam's spirit, keeping him from his dreams.

"Okay." Adam didn't sound unhappy, but Kano bit back a growl nonetheless. It was like there was no middle ground.

The instant Tim disappeared, Kano moved to his office door and turned the lock. Adam's smile immediately transformed, turning genuine and mischievous. "So, is Rylan really late or was that a ploy to have me alone?"

A chuckle sneaked out. Kano loved having the real Adam. It never failed. Each time Kano thought to get the man alone and demand Adam explain why he kept shutting Kano out, the moment would come when they were alone, and Kano couldn't hang on to his anger. "Sarah alerted me of Rylan's arrival thirty minutes ago."

"I can't imagine it'll take Tim long to figure out you lied."

Kano shrugged. "Tim is a smart guy. He'll recognize I wanted him gone and stay that way for a while."

"Kano..."

Kano knew that tone. Adam was about to lecture him on being the boss and risking Adam's reputation. Kano shut it down before it started. "They're sleeping together, so I'm sure Tim will be more than happy to hang around until Rylan finishes up. No doubt they already have a coat closet picked out downstairs."

Adam's mouth hung open. "Shut up." Kano wondered if Adam heard the gossipy tone to his voice. "Tim and Rylan? Shut. Up."

Kano nodded. "They think I don't know. I always know everything."

"But Rylan's so evil," Adam said, sounding scandalized.

Closing the distance between them, Kano came to stand over Adam. Two weeks after Kano had hired Adam, he'd purchased a plush loveseat and laptop as Adam's workstation for odd jobs. Kano intended to find out if the comfy-looking piece of furniture could handle some abuse. "I imagine that's part of the appeal for someone as alpha as Tim. He isn't one to put up with much while Rylan would get bored of anyone he could walk on within a week."

Adam set his laptop aside, giving Kano his full attention. "Still," Adam said, "I can't picture it."

Kano helped Adam to his feet. "That's good. Right now, you shouldn't be picturing them together. You should concentrate on what I'm about to do to you."

The way Adam's mouth lifted in one corner had Kano's stomach growling from hunger. "What are you about to do to me?"

Kano reached for the zipper of Adam's jeans. "I'm about to christen this loveseat by fucking you senseless on it."

"Promise?"

Adam's open challenge broke something loose inside Kano. In a matter of seconds, Kano had Adam face down on the couch with his bare ass in the air. He tore through his wallet, finding a lubricated condom. Kano had already learned to be prepared for these stolen moments, since he tried hard to capture as many as he could. Adam's deep moan came out sounding muffled with his face buried in the cushions. Kano's hands didn't stop shaking from want until Adam's tight heat squeezed him and pulled him deeper inside. Kano held still, trying to calm his racing heart while giving Adam time to adjust to the intrusion. In his heart, Kano knew what this was really about. He was trying to claim Adam and force the man to stop pretending they weren't real. Kano's heart couldn't tolerate the way Adam smothered him with affection at night, only to yank it away the next day. He needed to brand Adam as his.

"I don't want to do anything except be inside you," Kano admitted as he rocked against Adam. "I've been addicted to you since the first time we held hands." Kano couldn't stop with the confessions. "Your skin feels like it belongs against mine."

Adam stroked his cock, tightening his ass as he pumped. "I won't last if you keep talking and I don't want to get cum all over this couch."

Shit. Kano hadn't thought of that. His only concern had been getting inside Adam as fast as possible. Kano loosened his tie and unbuttoned his shirt. Once he had the piece of material in hand, he gave it to Adam. "Use this. I have more in the closet."

Adam shifted positions. His body went taut. Kano sucked in a harsh gasp. The man was so damn tight. Sometimes Kano worried Adam would break him. He could barely keep his eyes open from the pleasure of Adam's ass trying to pull him deeper. It was never about sex for Kano, but goddamn. He couldn't deny there'd never been anyone like Adam for him. In the past, Kano had been content with one night. If he never saw them again after that, all the better. Adam had Kano enslaved. Pride demanded Adam find release first. His body didn't give two shits about Kano's ego. There was no reasoning with a looming orgasm. In the heat of the moment, there was nothing but the itch. There came a point when nothing could stop the need for release. Even if the building started falling down around them or a team of firemen burst through the door, Kano knew he couldn't stop until he found the bliss only Adam offered.

Adam's cell phone rang.

Kano cursed.

Adam's orgasm hit, convulsing on Kano's dick and making him lose his sight, hearing, and ability to talk. Ecstasy ripped through him, nearly taking his knees out. Kano clung to Adam, hoping he wouldn't fall and crush him. Pulses of electricity ran through Kano. His breaths came out in loud gasps. He wanted to ride the waves for the rest of the day. Love filled his chest, rising in his throat and choking him. This man was his. Kano always knew it in the aftermath of their lovemaking. In those moments, the knowledge was clearer than any other inside his mind.

"Jesus, Kano. How much did the shirt I just ruined cost?"

Kano touched his lips to Adam's nape. "Way less than I'd pay for just that purpose. Damn, Adam. Do you have some sort of sex-hating app on your phone that calls you when we get too close?" Adam's laughter felt good against Kano's skin. He didn't want to release Adam, but he couldn't keep the man pinned to the loveseat all day. The instant Adam was free to do so, he spun and slammed his mouth over Kano's, delving his tongue inside. The sensation of love choking him increased. He could never get close enough to Adam to soothe his heart.

"Oh yeah," Adam hummed against Kano's lips. "That's what I've been waiting on," he said before deepening their kiss once more and entwining his tongue with Kano's. "I love the way you taste," Adam admitted as he changed angles and went back for more. This was the side of Adam that Kano craved nonstop. In these moments, he knew he mattered as much to Adam as Adam meant to him. Other times, he wasn't so sure. He hated those other times.

For a moment, Kano pulled Adam as close as he could get him. They touched from sternum to thighs. His hands brushed every inch of skin he could reach. When it couldn't be avoided any longer, Kano pulled away. He met Adam's stare. "Tonight, you'll stay with me. I'll run us a hot bath and we'll soak until the water is ice cold. By the time I take you to bed, you'll beg for mercy. I haven't decided yet if I know the meaning of the word." He felt Adam shiver. A smile that felt evil even to him stretched Kano's lips. "Check your phone. It might be important."

Adam did as Kano said, but he still looked dazed. "It's Jace," Adam said unnecessarily. No one else ever called him as far as Kano knew. Adam readjusted his clothes as he called Jace back.

"Hello?" Jace's voice rang through the office.

"You're on speaker," Adam warned. He held Kano's soiled shirt and glanced around the room as if he had no idea what to do with it.

Kano relieved him of it and tossed it in the trash.

Adam looked horrified but didn't argue. Of course, that was most likely due to Jace's ability to hear anything he said.

"I'm so glad I caught you," Jace said, sounding panicked.

Kano's head whipped around. His gaze locked on the phone. "What's wrong?"

"I have a problem," Jace said, as if they hadn't already figured that out by his tone alone. "They've cancelled our flight back to Tennessee. We sat onboard for three hours before they announced they'd have to cancel due to operational reasons. They've rescheduled us for tomorrow, but I have the movers coming tomorrow to put our stuff in storage. The problem is, I haven't finished packing everything, and—per our deal—they won't take anything not packed and ready to go."

"Okay," Adam said, sounding like he was trying to keep up but not sure what any of this had to do with him.

"There isn't a huge amount of stuff that needs to be boxed up and it's not that big of a deal. What is a big deal is—there's no way we can be there before the movers show up."

"Yeah, that's a problem."

"So," Jace continued as if Adam hadn't said anything, "we were wondering, if we bought you a ticket, if you would fly down tonight, pack up the rest of the stuff, and hang out until the movers get there tomorrow. I really don't want to lose all the money we've spent on this. Not to mention, the couple renting the house are scheduled to move in three days from now."

Adam's gaze shifted Kano's way, as if seeking his permission. Kano quickly went over his schedule in his mind. "Don't worry over a plane ticket. I'll get Adam there."

Instead of looking relieved, Adam covered his eyes with his hand as if he couldn't believe what just happened.

"Oh," Jace said, sounding confused. "You weren't lying about me being on speaker. Is this Kano?"

Adam still wouldn't look at him.

"Yes. My driver will take us to gather a few things for the trip, but I should be able to have Adam there within three hours."

"Thank God," Jace breathed, sounding relieved. "Just let me know how I can make it up to you, and I'll do my best."

"No thanks needed. Adam has moved his schedule around many times—losing time with you—to ensure his availability for my schedule. I can do the same this one time."

"You have no idea how much I appreciate it. Adam, I'll see you as soon as I can tomorrow. Thank you for this. Tyler and I will pay you back for any time you miss from work."

"It's not a problem," Adam said. His voice sounded normal, but his features were hard.

As soon as the call disconnected, Kano tried to get Adam to look at him. It didn't immediately happen. "Are you okay?"

"Fine," Adam said, gathering his things. "I guess we should hunt down Tim."

Before his man could get away, Kano wrapped his arms around Adam's waist, giving him no choice but to meet his gaze. "If you're upset with me, say so."

Adam gave a short nod. "Stay here and let me go alone."

"No."

"Then I'm upset."

Despite the situation, a snort of laughter escaped Kano. At the sound, Adam smiled. They were okay. Adam might claim to be upset, but Kano knew him too well. Adam might be irritated over Kano's high-handed tactics, but his ire wouldn't last ten minutes.

"Your uncle needs you, but I promised you a bath."

Adam sighed. It was a tired sound. "You should've asked me before making such an offer."

"There wasn't time and you know it." Kano swiped his hand over the curve of Adam's ass as he said the words. Even he wasn't sure if the move was meant to soothe Adam's temper or because Kano couldn't resist touching his ass.

"I know," Adam admitted, but he didn't sound happy about it. "But you do tend to run roughshod over me at times."

Kano raised his eyebrows. "So no bath?"

Adam pulled out of his hold and growled, "You'll get your freaking bath."

With Adam not looking at him, Kano gave in to a smirk. Jace's flight getting cancelled couldn't have come at a better time as far as Kano was concerned. Maybe a little time away from this place and everyone would do them some good. He needed to take Adam away, where there were no prying ears or eyes. Where no one would hear him scream.

* * *

Adam had changed clothes when they ran by his apartment before leaving for Tennessee. Kano had refused to leave Adam's sight long enough to change, almost as if he expected Adam would run for the hills if he turned his back. He wasn't wrong. They were standing in Jace's kitchen. The kitchen from his childhood. In his home state, and Adam was still considering running for the hills. Kano wasn't the one at fault. Adam was. When he'd left home, headed for New York, Adam had been driven and focused. Since the first moment he'd set eyes on Kano, Adam hadn't looked away. Sometimes he thought if he could take a few days away from Kano's constant and sexy presence, he would find his drive again. Come up with a solid plan for his future. Right now, all Adam saw was Kano. Perhaps that was all the answer he needed. Maybe Kano was his future and this feeling of listlessness would vanish the moment he accepted it. But it was as if Kano didn't want him to take that breath.

He'd never been more torn in his life. All the dreams Adam had before meeting Kano still ate at the back of his mind, but he'd lost sight of how to achieve them. Not to mention, now that he was seeing Kano, he wasn't sure if anyone would take him seriously again or if his merit would count for anything. What if people chose him for their events, as Tamara had done for her wedding, only because of his connection to Kano? Adam's biggest fear was he'd never feel like he'd accomplished anything because he couldn't believe he'd earned it.

On the other hand, did he care? As long as he was doing what he loved, did it matter how he'd gotten there? Adam would care the moment Kano dropped him because he'd come too easily to the man. A growl sounded loud in Adam's head. He was confused with no relief in sight. Adam wanted to crawl out of his skin to get away from his thoughts.

Adam tried concentrating on the mundane instead. Jace had been right. There wasn't much left to pack, but he could see why they wouldn't want to get stuck trying to get what was left boxed up and carried to storage before the new tenants moved in. Plus, he knew from checking prices when he'd moved to New York that moving companies were outrageous. While Jace and Tyler could afford the expense better than he could, Adam could still understand why they wouldn't want to risk losing what they'd already paid.

Kano's arms found Adam's waist. He pulled Adam back against his chest, hugging him tight. Adam's hands automatically went to the arms around him and held on. He needed Kano's hugs like oxygen. Adam's mind settled as he admitted the truth to himself that he'd been skating. He had nothing to offer. Any day now, this amazing man would wake up and wonder why he was with Adam when he could have someone perfect and successful. Adam was no one. He was an assistant. How long would it take for Kano to figure that out? Losing this person who'd come to be his whole world would kill Adam, and he didn't think he was being dramatic. If Kano left, he'd take all the air with him, and Adam would slowly fade away.

"I've checked all the rooms. It looks as if most everything is already packed. What little that needs doing won't take long at all. One thing I noticed, there's no place to sleep. All the bed coverings are packed already, as well as towels and dishes. What do you say we find us a nice hotel with room service after we're done?"

Adam turned his head and pressed a quick kiss to Kano's cheek. "Sounds good to me as long as we're back before the movers show up tomorrow morning."

"Punctual is my middle name."

"Really?" Adam asked while trying to pull Kano's arms tighter around his waist. "I thought it was Smoking-Hot. Kano Smoking-Hot Aramante."

Kano's body shook with laughter. His lips touched Adam's shoulder, making Adam's eyes fall closed from the weight of his emotions. "I don't have a middle name, so I'll take it."

Adam spun in Kano's arms and met his stare. "Seriously? Who doesn't have a middle name?"

"Lots of people," Kano said. The way his eyes swam with humor made Adam suspicious.

"Are you screwing with me?"

Kano shook his head. "I'm being quite serious. My great-great-great-grandfather was the last Aramante to have a middle name. He thought it to be bad luck, since his brother didn't have one and was much more successful. Since then, no Aramante has given their child one."

"Well, he must've been right. Look how successful you are."

"Honestly, I think it's a bit of a trade-off in our family," Kano admitted. He pulled away and grabbed a box. While taping the bottom closed, he continued. "It seems, in my family, you have one or the other. You're either successful in love or money, but never both. Take my parents as an example."

"They don't strike me as loving," Adam said, interrupting. He immediately regretted the words. If the shoe was on the other foot, he wouldn't like Kano talking badly about his family. Adam winced. "Sorry."

"Don't be," Kano said, setting the box aside. "They've never cared much for Nina or me. In truth, I think we're a bit of a bother to them. You see, you couldn't tell it at lunch because we were arguing, as usual, but they're madly in love. Even after forty years of marriage, they can be a tad sickening. Growing up, I think Nina and I were in the way of them being alone. I've always believed they thought they wanted children until they had them and realized we took away from their time of being in each other's pockets."

Adam claimed the box Kano made and began to fill it with odds and ends. "That's sad, but not unheard of. My grandparents

180

were like that on my dad's side. They had seven children. I have so many cousins I wouldn't know them if I passed them on the street, but my mom used to say they never wanted that big of a family. They just couldn't keep their hands to themselves and didn't believe in birth control."

Kano's laughter kept Adam telling his ass.

"That's why she asked Jace to be my godfather. She didn't want me subjected to their hatefulness if anything happened to them, which, as you know, did happen."

"What of your other grandparents?" Kano asked, taping together more boxes.

"They were old as Methuselah before I was born," Adam said, making Kano laugh so hard no sound emerged. "If they'd taken me in, I would've had to go through two more deaths before I turned eighteen. Not that I didn't have to suffer through losing

181

my grandparents, but we weren't close. They went into a nursing home before I was old enough to understand who they were to me. So, really, they were just people Jace made me visit a couple of times a year on Sunday." The conversation turned serious before Adam intended. "Oddly enough, the day my grandfather passed away, is the day I started talking again after three years of resting my voice. I was officially all Jace had left in the world. We were sitting at the funeral home, waiting while they dressed him, and I realized if I didn't say something, all Jace would have was the hate-filled voice of his husband at the time, who was a horrible person. I didn't want that."

"That's because you're a good person," Kano said so quickly there was no way Adam could doubt he believed it was true.

Instead of arguing, since Adam wasn't so sure it was true, he chose to make light.

"You only think so because I cook for you sometimes."

Kano set the tape aside and moved closer. "And you make people feel good about themselves," Kano pointed out. "You may not think I'm paying attention, but I hear you when you're helping out around the set. I love it when you try to lift people up when they confide they don't like things about themselves. Not to mention, I thought I'd have to pull you off my father at lunch when the name calling began. You're fierce and brilliant."

While looking into Kano's eyes, Adam knew, Kano believed every word he said. Adam wanted to be everything Kano thought him to be.

*

There wasn't much packing to do, but Kano wanted it all done right then. The way Adam watched him, as if barely restraining himself from taking Kano to the floor, had Kano struggling for air. There was so much fire in Adam's eyes. Kano had never felt more desired, and not just sexually. Adam's stare said he was greedy to own all of Kano. This, all of this was what Kano had been starving for in New York. He craved the way Adam looked at him. The man gave Kano power he'd never known before him.

A knock landed on the door, tearing Adam's heated gaze away. He focused on the door. The lines marring his forehead let Kano know Adam hadn't been expecting anyone. He took a step toward the door and paused. Adam didn't seem to have any intention of opening it.

"Do you plan to answer that?" Kano asked, incapable of withstanding another moment of Adam's waffling.

With a shrug, Adam pulled the door open. Some woman he'd never seen before stood on the other side. She was thin and closer to Kano in age than Adam. Her brown hair was windblown, but her nails were perfectly manicured. Middle-class, Kano surmised.

She squealed when she set eyes on Adam. Kano cringed at the sound. "How long are you here for?"

Adam stepped back and allowed the woman inside. "Um. Just until we get all this squared away."

The woman's gaze swept the room. Her expression turned puzzled as she eyed the bare walls and mounds of boxes before focusing on Kano. "I feel like I'm missing a lot. Who is your friend?" she asked, directing her question at Adam without tearing her gaze from Kano.

She was rude. Kano hated rude people. He answered for Adam. "Kano Aramante, and you are?" He let the question hang in the air. Even he heard the disdain in his voice, but it was out of his control. Kano had come here, intent on having Adam alone, away from the pressures of work. Adam needed to see there was nothing standing between them other than what he'd built in his mind. This woman was intruding on their time.

"Paige Carpenter," Paige said, clutching her purse tighter. As if the move didn't prove his gut feeling about her, she kept talking. "What is a man of your... stature doing here—alone—with someone as sweet as Adam? I can't think Jace would appreciate that."

Kano felt his face harden. Adam already had his own doubts about Kano without this woman insinuating Kano was an old man intent on molesting a child. Adam was old enough to take care of himself. He'd more than proven that over the last few months. Kano could destroy her, but didn't have the time. Instead, he held on to his calm. "I'm helping Adam pack."

Paige smirked.

Kano narrowed his eyes, rethinking his strategy. He could destroy her and still make time for Adam.

Her evil smile didn't abate, even with Kano giving her his best death stare. "Dressed like that?" she asked, pointing out Kano's expensive suit before motioning toward Adam's ragged jeans and worn out T-shirt. It was true Adam was dressed for the chore of packing up Jace's things while Kano was not. But, then again, Kano had money. He could pay people to take care of this. Without his permission, Kano's voice turned condescending. "I don't have to get my hands dirty to help anyone do anything."

Paige sneered at his tone.

Adam intervened. "Did you need something, Paige?"

She turned away from Kano,

dismissing him.

Kano bit back a snort. She was weak. If he leaned on her, she'd cave. The problem was—Kano wasn't so sure that would win him any points with Adam.

"I came by to speak to Jace, but I wasn't expecting all this," she said, motioning toward the boxes. "Since we don't work together any longer, we don't speak as much as we used to. In fact, it's been so long, I've lost his number. You know how it is. I got a new phone and all my contacts didn't transfer. Is Jace moving?" she asked, eyeing the boxes once more.

Adam dug his phone out, obviously intent on handing over Jace's personal information. "I've got his number."

Kano set his hand over Adam's, stopping the motion. Adam's head jerked up, as if he intended to put Kano on blast. The irritation written in his every line disappeared when his gaze met Kano's. He knew Kano well enough to know he wouldn't interfere unless he had a good reason. Something was off about this woman. He couldn't sit idly by and allow Adam to give her access to Jace. "Jace hasn't been here since the day he called to tell his boss he wouldn't be back. Even I know that, and I've never met the man." Only because Adam flat-out refused to let Kano meet his uncle. Kano hadn't decided yet if it was due to their age gap, or if it was one more way he kept Kano at arm's length. "It seems strange you'd show up here on the exact day someone is here. I'm not much on coincidences." If she was in any way stalking Adam, he would end her.

"I told Jace I would keep an eye on the place," she said, deflecting, but there was a definite cagey look in her eyes. "As I was passing by, I saw a light on."

Adam shoved his phone in his back

pocket again, making Kano proud.

Kano wasn't finished tearing her down. "Do you live in this neighborhood?" He knew she didn't. Houses here were worth more than this woman made. He knew his designers. She wasn't dressed to suit this lifestyle. Kano wasn't being snobbish. He didn't care how much anyone paid for their clothes as long as they wore them well. This was about this woman's shady behavior, and her attempts to use Adam for whatever she was trying to pull.

Paige shifted from foot to foot. "No."

"So, you were driving by, through a gated community, to check on a friend's house, who even you admit you haven't spoken to in so long you no longer know how to contact them?"

Paige's shoulders squared, letting him know she wasn't backing down. That was okay. Kano had her number. "I don't know you. It's none of your concern what arrangement I have with my friend."

Kano pulled out his phone. "I would feel better if I spoke with my friend at the Justice department before Adam hands out any personal information. As you pointed out, I don't know you. For all I know, Jace has a restraining order against you and you shouldn't even be here." Kano focused on Adam. "While I'm doing that, you should probably go ahead and call the police to be safe."

Adam's mouth fell open as Paige scrambled for the door. She scratched at the knob as if stuck in a horror film with a killer on her heels. Once she made it through the door, she was gone. Adam stared at the spot where she'd been standing. Kano couldn't stop staring at him. A low chuckle escaped him before Kano could call it back. Adam's surprise was adorable.

Adam pressed a hand to his stomach. Kano's gaze locked on the telling motion. He might try to pretend he didn't feel as much for Kano as Kano felt for him, but Adam did. The problem was—Kano didn't know how to make Adam admit it.

Adam dropped his hand and met Kano's gaze. The desire written in Adam's every line had Kano's stomach tying in knots.

"Do you really know someone at the Justice Department?"

Kano snorted. "Not only do I not know anyone, I'm not even certain what they do, but I recognize crazy from a mile away. Stalkers flock to me. That woman had 'nutter' stamped all over her." He'd been in the US for years, but still didn't totally understand the difference in their departments, but as he'd said, crazy he understood on every level. Like the sort of insanity Kano felt every time he considered the possibility Adam would never fully be his. Even so, he would never let anything happen to the man. "Aren't you glad I ignored you when you told me not to come here?"

Adam licked his lips. Kano's gaze dropped to Adam's mouth. He could kiss him now and distract him from their chore. Most likely, Adam would let it happen. Desire roared through him. He'd never wanted to savor anything like he did Adam's flavor. Still, Adam clung to his pride.

"No. As always, I would've been fine without you."

A low laugh escaped Kano. He wondered if Adam realized how breathless his denial sounded. He closed the distance between them. Adam didn't back away. Kano's boldness grew. Before he could stop himself, Kano cupped Adam's cheek. He brushed away the moisture left behind

193

on Adam's bottom lip. His stomach cramped with the desire to bring his thumb to his mouth and suck away Adam's flavor. They were more than Adam gave them credit for being. Adam knew all he had to do was tell Kano to go away, and he would. Kano would never push himself on Adam if Adam didn't want him, but Adam did want him. They had a connection Kano couldn't deny. He would never allow any harm to come to Adam.

"I don't need your permission to protect you, Adam. I always take care of what's mine." Adam didn't deny Kano's claim. It was a win as far as Kano was concerned. He took a step back. "Point me in the direction of where you'd like me to start."

"That was some sexy alpha chest beating you had going on just then. I think you need to start right here," Adam said, tapping his lips.

Kano didn't need to be told twice. In a single stride, he overcame Adam and captured the man's mouth. Their tongues met and retreated before entwining. They fought to get closer. Erections bumping. His lips stung from Adam nipping at them. They were wild and Kano wanted all of it.

After tearing his mouth away, Kano fought to catch his breath. His lungs burned from the effort. "Let's get this finished," he begged. "Once I start peeling off these clothes, I don't want to stop. Let's get this packing out of the way. I need you to myself and undistracted."

Adam nodded against his shoulder. His breathing sounded every bit as labored at Kano's. "Agreed. I want to take my time."

Kano's knees weakened at Adam's confession. He was one night of Adam's undivided attention away from falling on his knees and begging Adam to never leave him. The man had ruined him for anyone else, but this—all this—was what had been missing for Kano. This open lust from Adam. He'd craved feeling desired the same way he craved Adam. It was even better than he expected. Hunger consumed his brain. The same greed he'd felt when he'd started *Today's Beauty* overcame him once again, but for a new target. As quickly as the longing hit, so too did the fear. There was a single truth in his mind Kano couldn't shake. The moment they went home, and Adam ripped this affection away again, Kano might do anything. He'd never been more frightened of himself than he was in that moment. Kano might take a match to the world if it stood between him and having this version of Adam.

* * *

They made it back to Jace's with a half

hour to spare before the movers were set to arrive. Adam had hoped for at least an extra hour. He'd wanted to do one final sweep, ensuring they hadn't missed anything, since they'd been in a hurry to leave the night before. His hopes had died a fiery death when Kano joined him for his morning shower. Goosebumps rose on his skin and butterflies stirred in his gut as Adam remembered the gentle way Kano held his jaw, forcing Adam to hold his stare as Kano took him against the shower wall. Those steel eyes hadn't wavered, forcing Adam to accept Kano's domination. His phone chimed, pulling Adam out of his daydream of being in Kano's arms.

Jace: *We'll be there in a few. You're free to go if you need to get back to work.*

Adam: *I'll stay, and at least get a hug before I go.*

Plus, Adam was finally ready for Jace and Tyler to meet Kano. He was nervous as heck, but the truth was—Adam loved Kano. Maybe Adam didn't know where they were headed and was still scared to death of Kano crushing him, but he could give Kano this much.

Jace: *Yay! We'll see you in a minute then.*

Adam moved from room to room, searching for any odds and ends they'd missed, before rejoining Kano in the kitchen. Once again, Kano was overdressed. Adam had to take a deep breath to control his body's reaction to the sight. He pressed his hand to his stomach, hoping his obsession with Kano didn't show in his eyes.

"Jace texted me and said they'll be here any minute."

Kano turned at his words. His face was an emotionless mask. A sick sense of dread rose inside Adam for no reason at all. There was a cool vibe in the air that hadn't been there before.

"I'll let the pilot know to get ready," Kano said, sounding as cool as the air, as he pulled his phone from inside his jacket.

Adam waited until Kano finished sending his texts before losing the battle with his nerves. "Is something wrong?"

At his question, Kano tore his gaze away from his phone and focused on Adam. His face softened. Adam's shoulders relaxed. It had been all in his head. "Not wrong, no," Kano said, immediately setting Adam on edge again. He couldn't breathe. This was what was wrong with their relationship. Kano had all the power. Adam was just a mess, waiting for Kano to discard him. "Listen,

I've been thinking," Kano said, slipping his phone back in his pocket.

Jesus. Those were the worst words on the planet. Adam wondered if he'd faint. "And?" Adam had no clue how he sounded so normal.

Kano moved a step closer. "I think we need to talk."

Adam had been mistaken. *Those* were the worst words on the planet. "Okay."

"It can wait until we're in the air and have time, since Jace will be here soon."

Maybe Kano was fine to wait. Adam couldn't. "No. We have a minute."

The way Kano's shoulders heaved as he took a deep breath struck fear in Adam's heart. He knew then he'd hate whatever fell from Kano's lips. "You're different here."

Adam nodded. He couldn't deny it. Here, he felt free to love Kano. In New York, he'd go back to being Kano's assistant. No longer free.

Kano closed the last bit of distance between them and rubbed Adam's arms, as if he could sense Adam barely holding together. The move made Adam realize goosebumps covered his skin. He was half a second away from shaking like an abused dog from the chills running down his spine.

A sad smile touched Kano's lips, making things worse. "I've known for a while something wasn't one hundred percent right between us, but this trip has shone a spotlight on the issue. The thought of getting on that plane and heading back to New York makes me sick, because I can't go back to feeling like I feel when we're there."

That stiffened Adam's spine a hair. He might not like their circumstances, but he loved Kano all the time, not just here. "How do you feel there?"

Kano didn't pull any punches. "Like you only dole out affection when it's convenient. You only want me when you want me, and then you hold me at arm's length."

The worst part of Adam's anger was he knew Kano was right. He did everything Kano accused him of doing. Adam had his reasons and they were valid. In the face of Kano's pain, he couldn't think of an argument. All he felt was... pissed off. "You're my boss." It was literally the one and only argument Adam could dredge up in the midst of his rage. Most of his fury was aimed at himself, but he couldn't change how he felt.

Kano nodded. His understanding did

nothing to cool Adam's temper. "I know, and I get that. That's why I think you should move in with me."

"What?" The word fell from Adam's numb lips, sounding every bit as furious as he was.

Kano nodded again. "If we're living together, and everyone knows it, then there's no reason for you feel like we have to hide." Kano smiled. It looked hopeful and ripped out Adam's heart. "I want to hold your hand and tackle kiss you whenever I like. It was my hope you'd want those things too."

"But I don't," Adam said before he could stop himself. "This isn't what I want at all," Adam said, exploding into a full-blown rage and setting a match to his life. "I don't want to be that guy who everyone talks about, and for nothing good. We'll always be the couple where I went after my boss's money and landed him. It doesn't matter if it's not true. No one will ever believe I love you for you. They'll never see me as anything but a guy who snagged a sugar daddy. I want to be respected for my work ethic. No one at work will ever respect me after this."

Kano's expression gave nothing away. "Do you love me?" Kano asked, making Adam realize how much he'd confessed. He was all in now, laying waste to everything.

Adam growled, "Keep up, Kano. Of course I'm in love with you. Do you think I'd torment myself for anything less? If I didn't love you, I wouldn't care what people thought. I'd take whatever you offer without a qualm."

Kano shook his head. "That's bullshit. You're not that kind of person."

"How do you know? Hell, I don't even know if I am or not. I've never been put to the test. Being with you, it's consumed me from the very first day, and now I've loved you so long I don't remember what it's like to not love you. How can you ask me to be the guy who nobody thinks feels anything for you? How can you ask me to cheapen this?"

"How can you ask me to pretend I didn't hear you confess to loving me?" Kano said, taking Adam by surprise by matching his level of anger. "Tell me what you want from me, Adam," Kano demanded. "Not what you want from Kano Aramante. What you want from me," he said, tapping his chest.

It was the first time Adam could swear he saw Kano's heart. Adam was hurting him, but he didn't know how to make it stop.

205

Adam shook his head. "I can't."

The pain in Kano's eyes deepened. "Coward," Kano spat, leaving Adam feeling the same as if Kano had slapped him.

Adam lashed out. "You don't understand. I can't tell you what I want from you, because you *are* Kano Aramante. There's no you *and* Kano; you are that public persona and nothing more. There's no man behind the mask. There's only Kano the powerful and Adam the disposable." Halfway through his rant, Kano's expression closed until Adam stared at the empty shell Adam had all but accused the man of being. He wanted to take it back. All of it.

Kano dipped his chin, his manner cool. "Very well, Mr. Melkin. Good luck to you. I hope your co-workers' respect keeps you warm." Without looking Adam's way again, Kano picked up his bag and headed for the door. Adam ground his back teeth, swallowing back his apologizes and pleas for Kano to stay. As Kano reached for the back door, it swung open, forcing Kano to step back to keep from getting hit. Jace and Tyler spilled inside. They stared at Kano, wearing matching confused expressions. "Jace and Tyler, I presume," Kano said, still sounding like his voice would freeze water.

Jace nodded. "And you are?"

"Kano Aramante," Kano said. "Nice to meet you. Sorry for the abrupt meeting, but I have a plane waiting for me. Congratulations on your recent marriage, even though I realize it's not so recent any longer. Good day." Without another word, and without giving Tyler or Jace time to respond, Kano stepped around them and disappeared through the door.

Adam stared at the plain white slab of wood, praying Kano would push it open again, proclaiming his departure as the cruel joke it was. It wouldn't happen, but hope was all Adam had left.

"That was Kano Aramante? The man you've been telling me about?"

Adam tore his gaze away from the door. He tried focusing on Jace, but for some reason, his vision swam. "Jace," Adam said, sounding hoarse even to his ears.

Jace raced forward. Concern etched his every line. "What's wrong? Are you okay?"

Adam floundered for the words he needed. The ones that would give Jace all he needed to fix whatever was strangling Adam. He tried taking a breath. Nothing happened. His nose stung and his eyes burned. Adam gasped again. His lungs burned from the effort of trying to breathe without Kano. Jace patted his arms and shoulders as if searching for injuries. Even Adam couldn't point to where it hurt. The pain was everywhere. Kano was done with him. It was all Adam's fault.

He focused on Jace, hoping his uncle's face would give him a grounding point. Finally, he managed to choke out the truth that was silently killing him. "Oh, my gosh, Jace. I think I screwed up. I've messed up everything."

Chapter 7

Adam walked to work. Thanks to Tim picking him up every day, Adam had missed the coldest part of winter. Now, there was a hint of spring in the air. Even the promise of longer days and blooming flowers couldn't lift Adam's mood. Not to mention, he wasn't sure he even had a job to go to. He planned to show up and hold his chin high. If they turned him away at the door, so be it. Adam would cross that bridge when he came to it.

Kano wasn't the type of person to allow his personal life to interfere with his business. Even so, there was nothing stopping him from firing Adam as quickly as he'd swept Adam into his amazing position with *Today's Beauty*. In his heart, Adam knew he hadn't earned that job. Wasn't that his biggest issue? Kano held all the cards. If people said Adam slept his way to the top, Adam couldn't necessarily deny it. Adam knew Kano wouldn't have given him that position if he hadn't been attracted to Adam. He hadn't earned it.

As he pushed his way through the front door of the magazine's home office, Adam wondered if he'd puke. He knew it was all in his head, but he swore everyone stopped to stare. Adam headed for the elevator. When the door slid open, he came face to face with Tim. The blond giant's normally smiling face was set in a hard line as his gaze landed on Adam.

"I've been sent to escort you to your new office."

It hadn't been his imagination. People had been staring. They'd already alerted Kano he was there. Adam swallowed. "New office?"

Tim nodded and motioned him inside the elevator. "You're on the tenth floor now."

Adam stepped onto the lift while hoping Tim didn't notice the way his hands shook.

"What's on the tenth floor?"

"You are," Tim said, sounding as hard as his features. Okay. Point taken. No questions would be answered. The elevator slowed to a stop. Tim glanced his way. "Margot Freeman will run through your new duties with you."

"All right," Adam said, deciding to close off his feelings. He'd known today wouldn't be easy, but he was a professional. Adam still needed to eat. He would take whatever Kano threw at him.

Before Adam stepped out, Tim set his hand on Adam's forearm, stopping him. When Adam met the man's gaze, Tim's hard mask slipped, showing the concern he'd been hiding. "You're wrong about Kano. He's more than the face of this company. That man has been alone for years, without even a family to love him. He loved you, and you spat on it."

It was a cruel blow because it was true. Adam took it in the chest. "I know."

Tim dropped his hand, setting Adam free, but not without a final jab. "You're a goddamn idiot for pushing him away."

"That's true also," Adam said, stepping out and leaving Tim behind. It didn't matter what the man thought of him. There was no way Tim thought less of him than Adam thought of himself.

*

His new job sucked. Maybe that was the point. Perhaps Kano hoped to punish him. He'd been shoved into a tiny office in the corner, given photos of all the upcoming edition's models, and been ordered to choose color schemes. No longer was he allowed to create. Now he was the person in charge of matching makeup brands with skin types and filling out forms in some crazy computer program. Adam was a living, breathing how-to manual for makeup artist dummies. There was zero chance of Adam crossing paths with Kano in his new position. Several times, he caught people whispering behind their hands as they glanced his way. The job wasn't a demotion. In fact, it came with a raise and some fancy title. Once again, he hadn't earned it. But now, instead of saying Adam slept his way to the top, people would claim he blackmailed his way into an even better position. No doubt he was now the guy who'd slept with the boss and been paid off with a great job when the boss was done with him. It didn't matter if that was what people were really saying. Adam had the story in his head. Everything was too much. When he'd come back to work, he'd been determined to corner Kano and talk things out. Now, it was obvious Kano was finished with

Adam's bullshit. Adam couldn't blame him. He'd given Kano enough to keep him interested but heartlessly withheld his affection. It didn't matter Adam hadn't realized what he'd been doing. He was still guilty.

That was why Adam spent his lunch break drafting his resignation letter. Since he felt certain this position hadn't even existed before Kano created it to give Adam a place to go out of his sight, he didn't expect anyone would miss him. After creating a generic letter for Human Resources, Adam drafted a more detailed email for Kano. He left it in draft so there was no chance Kano would see it before Adam was ready. With both letters complete, Adam headed for the door. He dropped the paper version in Human Resources' mail slot and headed home. Adam waited until after he called Jace, letting him know what he'd decided, before hitting send on the email for Kano. It was done. Everything was over. There'd be no more late nights. No more baring his soul. No more Kano. Everything was gone.

*

"Did you get Adam settled into his new position?" Kano made it all the way to the airport before asking. For him, that seemed like the gold medal of showing restraint. He'd been dying and swallowing the inquiry back for hours. Now, with Rylan within sight and his window closing to speak freely, he needed to know.

"Yes, sir."

Kano did a double take. As far as he knew, Tim had never referred to him as sir before. Unfortunately, Rylan was now within earshot and Kano couldn't ask what the hell Tim meant.

"Rylan, so glad you could join us on such short notice."

Rylan dipped his chin while holding on

to his perfectly practiced smile. "I'm always at your service, Kano. You know that."

Kano knew a single hair hadn't moved even as Rylan did; that was what Kano knew. He didn't know why that fact bothered him, but it did. There was just something about Rylan. Something fake— like he secretly hated everyone and hadn't shown his hand yet.

No one spoke again until they were in the air. Kano wasn't surprised Rylan waited until Kano couldn't throw him from the plane before broaching the taboo. "I admit I was surprised to get your call. It was my understanding Adam was now your personal artist."

"I've got Adam working on a special project." Even saying Adam's name burned Kano's throat.

Rylan's smile turned into a sneer. "Tired of him already? Pity. I do try saving my team from the heartache of having their dreams crushed by people like you, but I can't help everyone."

Tim glanced up from the game he played on his phone and focused on Rylan. "Ry, stay out of it."

"Bitch, I don't work for you. Go back to minding your business."

"But you do work for me," Kano said, using his most cutting tone, and forcing Rylan's focus his way once more. "As Tim says, you should stay out of it."

An ugly-sounding snort escaped Rylan. There was a cold edge to his whiskey-colored eyes. "But I don't—in fact—work for you. I work for me. Every day, I'm in a different town, working with a different celebrity. You don't own me and you can't break me, so maybe you should listen for once. From day one, I try dialing back my interns' personal style, making them as plain as possible. If they don't stand out, then people like you don't take notice. Do you think Adam is the first intern I've had plucked from my team to be some star's plaything?"

"I'm sorry to have disrupted your team," Kano said, keeping his tone bland and hoping Rylan would take his apology as enough to let things drop. He was wrong.

"You didn't disrupt my team. If you recall, I fired Adam. Do you know what would've happened if you'd simply let my decision stand?"

Kano's temper was slipping. It seeped into his words. "A nice man would've lost his biggest dream."

"Ha!" Rylan cried, startling Kano. "His dream was lost the moment you rushed to his rescue and labeled him talentless. Because of you, no one will ever give his work merit. He'll always be the guy who slept his way to the top, and when you let him go, no one will ever work with him again. If you'd let him go, when I tried setting him free, Adam would've wrapped his anger around him like a cloak and taken over the world. Instead, you did to him exactly what I was trying to save him from—becoming nothing more than a joke to everyone in this industry."

"This sounds suspiciously like jealousy to me," Kano said, openly showing his anger and hatred. They'd gone past the point of hiding their hostility.

Rylan sat forward, as if daring Kano to continue. "Tell me what I have to be jealous of. Where's Adam now? Let me guess, you have him stuffed away in a corner office somewhere, making a whore's salary, while you steal his ability to create beauty from him."

Rylan was still talking, but Kano couldn't breathe. The man was so dead on with every word he said, Kano hated himself to the point of no going back.

As if clueless to Kano's inner war, Rylan leaned back in his seat and focused on Tim. The move made Kano wonder if Rylan was so sickened by Kano he couldn't look at him any longer, even as he continued his lecture. "Do you know what's wrong with people like you?" Rylan asked, but he didn't wait for Kano's answer. "The world is your oyster. That's fine, but once you've plucked and savored, do you know what's left of that oyster afterward? Nothing but an empty shell. I was never worried over me," Rylan said quietly. "No one can dim my shine, but my interns, they need protection from people like you." Tim looked up from his phone and focused on Rylan, hanging on the man's every word and making Kano feel as if Rylan was no longer talking to him. "I don't need you at all," Rylan added, sounding as if the wind had gone from his sails. Tim and Rylan stared each other down, wearing matching angry expressions.

Kano's phone dinged, saving him from dealing with Rylan for a moment. He checked his notifications. There was an email from Adam. Kano scrambled to open it.

Kano,

Thank you for not immediately throwing me out in the street, but I can't accept this new position. I've already turned in my letter of resignation to human resources. The past six months of working with you have been amazing. When I came to New York, I had a dream and a huge opportunity. Now, it's a corner office and dead feeling inside. This was never about money or position to me. I wanted to paint beautiful masks for people to hide behind, so they could have the confidence needed to create whatever dream they had for themselves. Since accepting your offer, I've done nothing to feed my soul. Better I should work in a department store, giving old ladies makeovers, than what I've been doing—pining for you and everything else out of my reach.

Kano had to stop himself from tossing his phone away. He didn't want to read another word. He'd honestly believed he was helping Adam. All the ways he'd failed kept burrowing under his skin and eating at his brain. Nonetheless, he couldn't stop reading Adam's words. Adam's next claim stopped him from destroying a perfectly good phone.

Mostly, I need to leave here because I can't lose you. When I got here today, I'd planned to corner you and beg you not to walk away from us. Give me another chance. Instead, you proved me right. You can put me back in my place any time you like. I love you. I realize I should've said that a thousand times by now. If you can't ever forgive me for stealing that from you, I understand. Just don't hate me because I don't want to be your whore. I know you never saw me that way, but the world does, and you made me feel like it was true today.

Kano's eyes fell closed and his throat tightened. Never in a million years would he have intentionally made Adam feel that way. When Adam had given Kano his virginity, Kano had felt the weight of that gift. He'd also felt clean and renewed—like Adam was this new beginning he hadn't realized he needed and would never squander. But he had. The first time he felt the least bit betrayed by Adam, he'd hid him away. Out of sight, but never out of mind. He didn't know how to fix it. Kano focused on the letter. He would start by reading every word Adam had written. Kano owed him that much.

I'm so sorry for every single time I ever held you at arm's length. You deserved so much more from me. For what it's worth, Jace has known about us since our last trip to London. I know that was a sore point for you. In truth, I wasn't entirely certain how he'd react to the news, and I didn't want to put you in the middle. Since he's as amazing as I've always claimed, he wouldn't stop digging until I admitted I'm in love with you. His support was as unwavering as always. After you stormed out, Jace said I was a lucky man. Not only are you incredibly sexy with an amazing accent, you also have fire. Even though I know all those things are true, those are Jace's words. He thinks you'll keep me hooked. Kano, he's right. I've been completely infatuated since the first moment we met, and I didn't know who you were. All I saw was a gorgeous man who made my heart race—not Kano Aramante who owns the world. Since then, I've learned you are smart, funny, kind, and passionate. I don't want to lose you. I don't know how to keep you.

If you never speak to me again, I get it. I deserve it, but I do love you. That was always true. —Adam

Kano read through the email twice more because he missed the hell out of Adam. He'd gotten used to having the man constantly at his side. His chest hurt. Now, all Kano had was Tim, who was obviously unhappy with Kano as well, and Rylan. The hatred went both ways with that guy. Adam had been the only light in Kano's day. Since they were mid-flight and Kano couldn't text Adam, he replied to the email.

I don't want to lose us either. You have no idea how sorry I am for everything. I shouldn't have left or tried hiding you away afterward. Right now, I'm on my way to Dallas. I don't know how to fix things, but when I get back, I want to try. You won't be happy working for me. I get that, but will you be happy working at a department store, giving old ladies makeovers? Or will you still feel there's a gap between us you can't fill? It drives me mad you can't see that I don't care what people think or if you match my income. Money is just money, while you're everything. I can't change what other people think, but neither can I stop needing you. If you would've told me what you wanted me to do to meet you halfway, I would've done it already, but you never talk to me. Tell me what you want from me. As long as you're not asking

me to get out of your life, I'll do my damnedest to give you what you need. —
Kano

Kano held his breath, waiting for Adam's response. When it came, Kano's vision blurred. He had to blink to clear the haze.

I just want you.

"When we get to Dallas, I would like for you, and Rylan if he's willing," Kano purposely spoke to Tim as if Rylan wasn't sitting there, "to go to the set in my stead. Please let them know I have an emergency to tend to back in New York. Rylan may handle my interview if he so chooses since he's every bit as versed in today's fashion. Either way, please let the pilot know we'll be returning to New York as soon as you disembark."

Without a word, Tim moved to do as he'd been told. Kano stared out the window, watching the clouds pass. He could feel Rylan watching him. Kano couldn't work up a care for the man's thoughts. His career meant nothing. The magazine meant nothing. Without Adam, none of it meant anything.

*

Someone was beating on his door. Adam found his Taser before moving to check the peephole. With Kano in Dallas, Adam didn't know who he'd call if someone was intent on breaking in.

The police, dumbass.

Funny how the thought not only hadn't occurred to him, it didn't soothe him the way having Kano come to his rescue did. Adam quickly checked the peephole, as if doing so put him in danger. His heart slammed against the wall of his chest when caught sight of Kano standing on the other side. He was supposed to be hundreds of miles away. How was he here? Adam threw open the door with more force than necessary.

Kano's gaze dropped to the Taser in Adam's hand. "I know you're upset, but really?"

Adam hid the weapon behind his back.

A smile lit Kano's face. "Sorry, love. That doesn't ease my mind. I didn't know you had it the last time you got me."

Adam tossed the Taser to the floor. The instant it was gone, Kano took two steps. Adam met him halfway. When Kano's arms engulfed him, Adam felt the first tear fall. He was such a weakling, but he was in love with this man and he thought he'd lost him forever.

"You're such a freaking horse's butt," Adam spat while still hanging on to Kano for dear life. "How could you leave me in Tennessee with no way to get back to you, and then run away before I had a chance to say I'm sorry?"

Kano snorted. "Horse's butt."

"Ass. There. Does that make you feel better?"

The arms surrounding him tightened. "No. You're right. That was unnatural coming from you." Kano took a step, forcing Adam farther inside the apartment before kicking the door closed behind him. He never let go. "I never meant to hurt your reputation. It never occurred to me I would," Kano admitted. "I thought if I loved you hard enough, it would eventually be enough to soothe whatever fears you had."

The tear situation was getting worse. Adam burrowed deeper into Kano's hold. "You love me?"

Kano pulled far enough away where he could hold Adam's gaze. He cupped Adam's face, ensuring he couldn't look away. "Baby, I love you so much I can't think. I question every move and decision I make, because I'm scared off my arse of

231

losing you. You can't be done with me. My heart can't take it."

"You never said anything." Adam sniffed, trying hard not to cry. "I didn't think you'd ever love me. Oh my God, Kano. I said the worst things to you. I love you and I said the worst things."

"Shhh," Kano soothed, touching his lips to Adam's. Adam sucked in a stuttered breath at the contact. He'd thought they'd never touch again. They'd never kiss.

Adam scratched at Kano's clothes, trying to get closer. "Take this off," he begged, tugging at Kano's jacket.

Kano shed the horrible piece of clothing standing in the way of Adam getting closer. Thankfully, Kano didn't stop there. He loosened his tie and ripped the buttons from his shirt as he fought to peel away the material between them. Adam whipped his shirt over his head before tossing it to the floor. Once they were bare from the waist up, they came together once more. Adam sucked in a hiss as Kano's warm skin met his. They were perfect together, melding into one another like puzzle pieces clicking together.

"Adam," Kano whispered between kisses. "Let's go to bed. I need to hold you."

Kano admitting he needed anything had Adam's feet moving. He held Kano's hand as he led the man toward his bedroom. Unlike Kano's huge king-sized bed, Adam only had a full-sized mattress. At least he knew Kano wouldn't go far. Despite Adam's earlier scramble to get closer, they stood beside the bed and took their time undressing each other. Adam took every opportunity to caress Kano's body. They stole kisses. Whispered words of love filled the otherwise silent bedroom.

The bed cradled his body as Kano

eased him down before covering his body with his. Their mouths clashed. The world, which had been out of balance since Tennessee, righted itself with each kiss. Adam never dreamed Kano would love him. Now that he had Kano's heart, all the concerns he'd suffered disappeared. He no longer cared what anyone thought. To hell with everyone. They knew the truth. This was real. This was love.

Their erections slid against each other. With his weight braced on one arm, Kano reached between them and palmed their cocks, stroking them at the same time. Adam gasped at the sensation of the friction between their dicks. There was no way Adam could walk away from this moment feeling anything other than he'd been made love to. There was a sweetness to Kano's touch. The slow way his hips moved, rocking into the pumping of their cocks, had Adam straining toward the oblivion Kano's touch promised. It wasn't about sex or release. This was a meeting of the souls. A promise for a real future. This was intimacy.

"I love you, Kano," Adam said, needing Kano to believe him.

Kano's mouth opened along Adam's jaw. "My baby. Love you so much," Kano said, melting Adam's heart as he set his skin on fire.

A gasp tore from Adam's lips as Kano's hot cum coated the sensitive nerve endings of Adam's crown. Kano's orgasm pulsed against Adam's cock. It was the hottest and sexiest moment of Adam's life. He would've sworn Kano had brought him to the peak of lust before now. Somehow, he'd taken Adam even higher. When Adam's orgasm hit, it was harder than any he'd experienced before. His body shook from the power of it.

"My god, Kano. Please don't ever leave

me again." He didn't care he was begging. There was no Adam without Kano any longer.

*

The sound of Adam's breathing and heartbeat kept Kano fascinated. It was funny how a few short days without Adam could leave Kano paralyzed with fear. If he closed his eyes, would this all be a dream? What if he woke up tomorrow and was in his bed? He might not ever get out of bed again.

"Adam."

At his name, Adam snuggled closer. "Yes?"

"Can I be frightened without you thinking I'm trying to control you?"

Adam rolled, facing him. His eyes sparkled in the dark. "I've never thought you're trying to control me. Why are you scared?"

"What'll you do if you're not working

for me? If you can't make ends meet here, where will you go? There's no home left for you to go back to with Jace gone."

He felt more than saw Adam shrug. "I'll work it out. With all our travels, I've made lots of connections. I'll think I'll do well on my own. Not to mention, you've been paying me way too much for six months now while also paying for everything when we're together. I have some money put away."

Kano chewed his bottom lip for a moment, wondering if it would be worse or better to tell Adam what he'd done. In the end, he needed to know Adam wouldn't struggle, even if something should happen and he never spoke to Kano again.

"If you find yourself in a bind, sell the nose ring I bought you for Christmas."

Adam released an outraged-sounding gasp. "Never. It's an adorable diamond and priceless to me because it's from you."

237

"Hmm," Kano said, wondering if Adam would kill him. "Um, well, that tiny diamond is worth seven hundred and fifty thousand dollars." Kano braced himself for Adam's explosion. To his surprise, silence met his confession. He couldn't take it. "Say something."

"Sweet Jesus," Adam breathed. "You let me walk the streets of New York, wearing a nose ring worth nearly a million dollars? Holy shit."

"Okay, cursing is super unnatural on you."

Adam sprang, catching Kano off guard. He straddled Kano's hips and got in his face. "Take it back. I can't keep it."

"No." In spite of Adam's anger, Kano wouldn't give in on this.

"You can't give someone that expensive of a gift."

Kano shrugged. "Yes, I can."

"Why would you do that to me?"

238

Adam was the only man alive who'd scoff at a gift. Kano needed to make Adam understand. He brushed his fingers through Adam's hair, trying to make Adam feel his love. "Because I love you," Kano said, trying to explain. "All I have is money. I'm not any of the things you believe. That night, at the mall, I took your hand without thought. When you didn't pull away, I glanced over and it hit me. I was in love with you and I had nothing to offer. I'm not funny or interesting. In fact, I'm not even that nice. All I could give you was material things. It was my bad luck money was the one thing you didn't want. Please," Kano begged. "Don't take away my ability to spoil you. No matter what you think of me, I don't agree. I need to have an outlet to justify you wanting me. Please?"

Adam didn't want to give in. It was written all over his face.

"Please, Adam?"

At his plea, Adam's shoulders fell. "Okay. I'll keep your gift. But in the future, you have to tell me if something cost that much. Don't let me walk around not knowing why I'm getting killed for my jewelry."

Kano's insides clenched at Adam's words. His grip automatically tightened on Adam's thighs. "I'll never let anyone harm you."

Adam didn't argue. He dipped his head and touched his lips to Kano's. "I'll never let anyone harm you either. You're mine."

Kano couldn't deny it. The moment he'd set his sights on Adam all those months ago, Kano hadn't stood a chance.

Chapter 8

So many people wished Kano happy birthday on his way to his office, he didn't think he'd make it there. He breathed a sigh of relief when the office door shut, closing him away from the chaos. He was tired of working up a smile he didn't mean. Every day, he got a little a more tired of working. Maybe it was time to step down? A gold box with a purple ribbon sat on his desk. Kano eyed it as he moved closer. Sarah wouldn't let just anyone in his office, and she hadn't mentioned a delivery. He snagged the tiny card on top and read.

Has anyone ever spoiled you? — A.

P.S. Pay close attention to the time.

His smile turned genuine as he lifted the lid from the box. The Breitling watch with the blue face he'd admired at Christmas stared up him. Kano didn't know how to feel. No one had ever bought him such a nice gift, especially someone who could least afford it. There was another note tucked beneath the watch.

Another delivery will arrive at the time set— A.

The watch was an hour fast. Kano sat down to wait. Part of him wanted to call Adam right then and chastise the man for spending so much on him. Another part of him wanted to call Adam and tell him how much he loved him. Afterward, he wanted to beg the man to drop everything and come to him. Waiting for the next delivery was the longest hour of his life. By the time the knock landed, Kano was ready to jump out of his skin. He raced to the door. A man in his mid-thirties shoved dozens of balloons into Kano's hands along with a note.

"Happy birthday," the guy said, sounding relieved to be rid of his burden.

He was gone before Kano recovered from his shock enough to offer a tip. Kano closed the door and ripped open his note.

These aren't for you. Take them to the second floor and hand them to a lady dressed in red. She'll give you your next gift. — A.

Kano chuckled. Jesus. Was this a gift or torture? He no longer knew. Being forced to walk through several offices and shove dozens of balloons into the lift before the door closed was a nightmare. Still, he couldn't stop smiling. On the second floor, he was relieved to find a woman waiting for him in plain sight. He shoved the balloons her way.

She handed him a small box. "Happy birthday." She too walked away without waiting for a response. Kano lifted the lid. There was a keycard to a high-end hotel he'd stayed at many times. A folded-up piece of paper was underneath. Kano unfolded it.

Tim is waiting downstairs to take you to your destination. — A.

BTW, happy birthday.

Kano pocketed the card and took the lift to the garage. Sure enough, Tim stood by the back door of his SUV, waiting.

He dipped his chin when he spotted Kano. "Are you ready?"

"Are you plotting against me now?" Kano asked before sliding in.

Tim smiled. "I'm plotting for you," he said as he closed the door.

It was a short drive even with the heavy traffic, but it still felt like forever. He'd never been more impatient. For all he knew, it could be another ridiculous errand waiting for him at the hotel. He prayed he'd find Adam there. Kano missed the man's face. The sound of his voice. Most of all, he missed the way he felt when Adam was in the same room—like he wasn't alone for the first time in years. Ever since Adam quit and started his own business, they didn't see each other anywhere near enough to suit Kano's heart. But, he'd gotten what he wanted. Adam was openly his. Fuck what everyone thought. Not that many people thought anything at all. Thanks to the beautiful work Adam had done, volunteering to help on sets while working for Kano, he'd made several connections. Everyone loved Adam and wanted him to make them beautiful. No one loved him as much as Kano.

After finding his room, the door easily opened once Kano inserted the card. He spotted a chilled bottle of champagne first and another present second. After a quick glance around, he swallowed down his disappointment. Adam was nowhere in sight. He moved to the couch and opened the box. It was filled with rose petals. He stared at them, wondering if he should dump them out to check for more clues or if this was a riddle he had to figure out by himself. Writing inside the lid caught his eye.

Dig.

Kano dove his hand inside and felt around. There was an envelope inside. He opened it, expecting anything at this point. Several items slid out. There were two plane tickets to Hawaii. They were for a commercial flight but first class. There was also a reservation for two weeks at an exclusive resort, starting tomorrow. Kano blinked at the dates, trying to mentally rearrange his schedule.

"Between Sarah and Tim, they cleared your calendar." Kano spun at the sound of Adam's voice. He stood in the doorway of the bedroom, looking like the sexiest man alive for no reason other than it was him. "Unless you don't want to go. I understand if you don't. It's not like I've given you much reason to want to spend any time with me at all lately."

Kano set the tickets aside and stood. "That's bullshit. I want any time you can spare for me, but you shouldn't have done so much for my birthday. It's just another day."

Adam shrugged, looking uncomfortable and unsure of himself. The sight melted Kano's heart. "Not to me, and this is nothing compared to what I wanted to do. If I could've afforded to put us on a private jet and travel the world until we were sick of each other's faces, I would've done so. You're always the one doing nice things for me. I always want to do the same for you."

Kano moved a step closer, wondering if Adam would let him touch him. Although things were better between them, he still had moments of insecurity in their relationship. "I've never wanted anything from you, except your time."

"That's not the point."

Kano moved even closer. "Then what is the point?"

Adam let out an exasperated-sounding sigh. "It's your birthday and I love you. That's all the point I need. I want to give you the world, even though you don't need it and can get it yourself." Adam's voice dropped to a whisper. "I want to be special—irreplaceable."

"You are," Kano said, finally managing to close enough distance between them so he could tug Adam into his arms. "Thank you, baby. This is the best birthday I've ever had."

Adam's arms encircled Kano's neck, making Kano's heart soar. "I'm not finished."

A chuckle escaped Kano as his hands found Adam's ass. "Don't bankrupt yourself. You have a new business to keep up."

"We still have to eat."

"Do we?" Kano asked. Even to his ears, he could hear the sexual invitation dripping from each word.

Adam nodded. "Eventually."

He wanted to play and talk. Damn, he'd missed Adam more today than usual, and that was saying a lot. Kano needed to bury himself inside this gorgeous man and never leave. Maybe then Adam would agree to be his forever. He held Adam tighter. "You are the most amazing man. Thank you."

"You don't have to thank me. I want your birthday to be perfect," Adam said against his chest.

"It was already perfect when I woke up this morning, because I have you." Kano tilted Adam's chin up, intent on capturing the man's lips. "I love you."

Adam blinked, as if fighting back

tears, and giving Kano pause. His voice came out low. "I never get used to hearing you say you love me."

Without warning, he popped the button on Adam's pants. "It won't ever be the last, because I love you more than air." He glanced down to where their bodies met. "Now, are there any more ribbons for me to untie or can I savor my present?"

The husky note to Adam's voice when he responded nearly crippled Kano. "There might be one or two ribbons. You should search me and find out, but not yet. I'm not finished spoiling you. You haven't had enough of that in your life."

Kano took a step back. He wanted Adam too much to keep holding him. "You got champagne," Kano said, tugging Adam toward the ice bucket and trying to give Adam his wish. If Adam wanted Kano to enjoy the gifts he bought first, that was what Kano would do.

"I did. It's cheap and sweet, so you'll probably hate it. I'm hoping you'll suffer through one glass so we can make a toast."

While keeping his gaze locked on his task, Kano popped the cork. He didn't bother checking the brand. As long as Kano had Adam, he couldn't care less about the taste of the alcohol. "What would you like to raise a glass to?"

Adam shifted nervously as Kano poured the champagne. "I hoped—if your offer to move in was still on the table—we could celebrate the beginning of our new life. If not, then we'll toast another year of your life."

"I'm sorry. It's not still on the table," Kano said, feeling like a complete dick. Adam moved as if to set the glass he'd picked up back down before pasting on a blatantly fake smile and hanging on to it, obviously intent on keeping his promise to toast Kano's birthday. Kano hated hurting Adam. This needed to be done. "After I left you behind in Tennessee, I thought long and hard about everything you said. What you want out of life, and what I want. I realized, we both want more than we gave ourselves credit for that day." Kano reached for Adam's glass. After relieving him of it, Kano set it aside, freeing Adam's hands. He held Adam's hands between his, forcing the man to meet his gaze. "You were struggling to find fulfillment working with me when you really wanted what you have now. I was fighting to hang on to you any way I could when what I really wanted was this," Kano said, dropping to one knee. Adam's eyes widened and his eyebrows tried hitting his hairline. "I know you hoped to surprise me with all of this, and you did. You're brilliant. But if you'd asked, I would've told you that the only thing I need is you. What do you say? Will you make my dreams come true and marry me?"

"Um."

Kano had known there was a real possibility Adam would tell him no. After all, the man hadn't hesitated to deny him when Kano had asked Adam to move in. This was important. Kano knew, in his heart, Adam would never stop feeling like Kano was out of his league unless they were married. Plus, he really wanted to marry Adam.

"Will my answer affect our relationship?"

Kano bit back a smile at the question. Adam always negotiated the terms before telling him no.

"No. If you say no, we can still move in together and it'll be like this moment never happened."

"Then, yes."

All Kano could do was blink. Surely he

hadn't heard Adam correctly. His man never gave in to anything without a fight.

"I said yes. You can get up now," Adam said, his voice laced heavily with laughter.

"I'm waiting for you to change your mind," Kano heard himself admit. "You never let me have my way."

"Please," Adam said, trying to pull Kano to his feet. "You always bully me into having your way. This one time you didn't, so I said yes on my own."

Kano refused to budge. "Now I want to stay on my knees for a different reason."

* * *

Q: *Tell us about the first time you met Kano.*
A: [With an adorable smile] *I was working the set of the annual holiday spread. Every time the elevator opened, I checked out the new arrivals. When Kano stepped out of the elevator, I couldn't look away. I didn't know who he was. He requested me as his*

artist. I'd never been more nervous in my life, because he seemed so much larger than life. While I was doing his makeup, our gazes met. Neither one of us looked away. My first thought was, "I'm going to marry this man." [Blushing] *I've never told anyone that.*

Kano set the issue of *Today's Beauty* aside. He couldn't take reading another line of Adam's interview without holding his man. It was too sweet and Adam's confessions had him falling even deeper in love, which was something he hadn't thought possible. With his head bowed, swiping samples of some new brand of makeup across his wrist, Adam was clueless to the danger lurking around him. Kano's hunger turned darker by the second as he stared at Adam. With the New York skyline behind him, Adam looked every bit the star he was.

"Come here." The growled demand sounded ominous, even to Kano's ears.

Adam glanced up. His features were clear of all emotion. Without question, he set aside his chore and crossed the room, coming to stand over Kano on the couch. His gaze never wavered. Kano's dick stirred. Having Adam's undivided attention was still his biggest weakness. "Are you feeling lonely over here by yourself?" Adam asked, as if he could read Kano's mind.

Kano didn't answer. In his head, all he could hear was Adam saying he'd known he'd marry Kano the moment they met. All the times Kano had thought how they were meant to be were proven by that one confession. He needed his other half right now.

"I need you," Kano said. His voice came out sounding hoarse. "Strip."

"What'll happen if I say no?"

An image of turning Adam over his knee filled Kano's mind. "You won't."

Leaning over, Adam braced himself against the couch on either side of Kano's head before going nose to nose with Kano. Defiance burned in Adam's eyes. "You're right," he said before covering Kano's mouth with his.

Kano's arms found Adam's waist. He pulled the man into his lap while deepening their kiss. Adam always kept him on his toes. He never knew if his sexy husband would give in without a fight or force him to take drastic measures. Either way, Kano was still the winner. In a time in his life when he hadn't known anything was missing, he'd met the other half of himself. Now, he'd spend the rest of his life a half-crazed mess, but at least he'd broken the Aramante curse. He was the first in generations to have love and money, but mostly love.

Keep an eye out for the next installment in the Hooked series.

Charity Parkerson is an award winning and multi-published author with several companies. Born with no filter from her brain to her mouth, she decided to take this odd quirk and insert it in her characters.

*2015 Readers' Favorite Award Winner
*Winner of 2, 2014 Readers' Favorite Awards
*2015 Passionate Plume Award Finalist
*2013 Readers' Favorite Award Winner
*2013 Reviewers' Choice Award Winner
*2012 ARRA Finalist for Favorite Paranormal Romance
*Five-time winner of The Mistress of the Darkpath

Connect with her online:

--Join my street team: facebook.com/TeamCharityParkerson

--Sign up for my newsletter: http://bit.ly/CharityNews
--Website: charityparkerson.com
--Facebook: facebook.com/authorCharityParkerson
facebook.com/TheMenofSin
--Twitter: twitter.com/CharityParkerso